Matt and the Magic Island

Chapters

Prolog

June 23rd, 2018, a flight leaves from Vegas and is headed to southeast Florida. A guy named Mike was on board, and so was a very young girl. The flight left Vegas at 10:30 and was expected to land in South Florida 4 hours later at 5:15. However, an hour after taking off, there is an unexpected landing.

In the center of the Gulf of Mexico, 1,000-miles away from the center part of the east coast of Florida. There is a magic island. The island is small at only 22-square miles and the island has not been discovered by anyone before, even geographers did not know of this island's existence. When the plane lands on the island, Two people, Matt, a man in his mid-20's and a young 18-year-old girl are trapped here after the plane they were on landed here due to technological issues, and missing their chance to get on the replacement plane.

After landing all 125 people on board were told that they would be there for 6 hours as a new plane was going to be on the way. Everyone else but Matt and a young girl stayed nearby and waited for their replacement plane to arrive. However, Matt and this girl felt adventurous and chose to explore this newfound land and in turn, missed there connecting plane that left the island at exactly the time the pilot had said.

So now without food, water, or shelter, they have become stuck on this island. None of them have good wilderness, survival skills, but Matt remembers a few that he was taught by his father and now must learn on the go to survive for God knows how long on this tropical island.

(As the two are stuck on this warm, beachy, palm tree jungle island nobody else, but the ones on that plane know this island exists. But let us back up a bit, how did these to get there?)

Ch One: Matt

Matt Hitten was born on June 26, 1995. He was raised by both of his loving parents. His father served in the Army until Matt was 12. So, they moved around the globe for some years. His mom was an ER nurse. Matt always excelled academically, especially in math. Matt graduated High school at an early age of 16 and studied at an Ivy League university.

Matt had recently finished college and graduated with two degrees, marketing, and finance. In the last year or so of his college days, he had a serious girlfriend. Matt and his college girlfriend were very much in love and they were together for almost a year and a half. However, as they were close to finishing school their different career paths separated them.

Matt got a job offer right after graduation at an investment firm called Millionaire Mile Investors in New York City after the firm heard about him from a company he interned for. Due to his work, they wanted him on their team. Deciding whether to take the job or not at first was a difficult decision. In the end, he decided to accept the offer, and he went.

The first few months at Millionaire Mile Investors was all about learning about the company, proving himself, and making the firm money, and Matt did that well. The firm worked with small size businesses that are interested in investing in the stock market. Matt got at least 7 companies a day to become new clients of the firm, which is better than most and which was very well noticed by management. By the time he was there for 6 months, he got promoted to office supervisor and it came with a raise. He was making about 20 percent more a month after being promoted.

Outside of work, Matt goes out a lot. Most times it is right after work with co-workers. Matt becomes a regular at a bar that is blocks away from where he lives. After a few months, Matt and a bartender become friends and they quickly start to hang out almost every weekend. After a few weeks, they become friends with benefits. Then within a few weeks, Matt and Venessa (the bartender at his regular bar) turn into something serious.

By the time Matt is at his job for a year, Matt becomes the assistant manager for the entire company and in charge of training. Matt is very excited about his new position. Matt and a few co-workers become friends after hanging out for some time, but there is one who Matt hangs out the most named Tayler.

Tayler is alone a lot and has been through a lot, and Matt tries to relate. Tayler is on his own and he is a new employee, also like Matt, he is relatively new to New York City. Although Tayler is making some decent money, Matt covers his tab most of the time when they hang out.

The first few times, Matt did not mind, but it soon got to a point where it was too much. Matt and Tayler were hanging out one night and when the bill came Matt said "Do you think we can split this down the middle?" Tayler said, "I can't afford even $5 right now." Matt replied, "I can't, nor do I want to hang out with you if I'm always needing to pay your bill. We have no difference in pay. Therefore, it doesn't make sense that you are always broke." Tayler replies, "Friends help each other out." Feeling annoyed Matt replies, "That is true, but not every single time and when have you helped me?" At the end of the night, Matt knew that his friendship with Tayler wouldn't last. So, that would be the last time they would hangout.

Meanwhile, Matt and Venessa's relationship grew and grew as they have been together for a few months, and they were delighted to be together. Venessa moved in with Matt after a year of dating. She continued to bartend a few nights a week, and Matt worked a lot at his office on Wall Street. They had a good time together and hung out at home a lot. At home, they wear little to no clothing as they both are into the nudist lifestyle. One time, when they both took 4 days off work; Matt and Venessa went to visit a nude resort.

The resort was in New York state near the center and about 125 miles from New York City. Being that neither one of them had a car, they just took a Lyft to and from the resort; however, it costs $130 each way. On their way to the resort, they stopped at a store to get their food and drinks, their Lyft driver accepted an extra $25 cash tip to wait for 20 minutes in the parking lot.

Matt and Venessa also did some traveling a couple of times through the years.

One trip was to France for two weeks. They got to do a lot of nudist stuff which they both enjoyed, and they did a lot of sight-seeing. France is home to a city named Cap d'Agde, this is an entire city near the water where you can go anywhere and do everything completely naked.

The couple spent 3 days living within this city. It was at the beginning of summer when they went, and it was around the time of their anniversary. The only thing about that trip they did not like is their long flight. Their flight was 13 hours one way and for them to drink they spent $125.

Their second trip was to Vegas towards the end of that same year. They had fun drinking and gambling. They hit every casino on the strip averaging 4 different casinos a day of the 4 days they spent there. Most nights, they got into their room around 11 at night, so they could spend alone time in their room getting drunk and being naked together.

Towards the end of the trip, Venessa got awful news from back home.

Venessa got the news that her father died the night before their flight back home, she became very depressed. She holds it together for a short while. Roughly 3 weeks of being back home and dealing with the loss, she falls into a very depressed state. It lasts for quite a while. She does seek help, but it only works for a short time. Soon her personality changes. After a month, she quits her job. Venessa shifts from becoming very depressed to becoming angry at every little thing. She also starts drinking very heavily and often to numb the pain.

Her father was her last living parent. Her father, she misses every day as she was very close to him as they use to talk every day. She knows Matt loves her, but she is so depressed to where she does not want to be loved by anyone anymore. Matt feels so bad for her and loves her a lot. Within a month, she gets hospitalized twice for suicide attempts.

Matt tries to stay with her by providing support and trying to convince her to get help. However, after 8 months of bad behavior issues and about 2 and a half years together, they broke up. The reason was that they argued too much, and it got to a point where they were getting violent. However, they stayed friends. And sometimes use each other for benefits.

Matt then decided to stay single for a few years, and he did. Matt continues to go a couple times a month to the bar where he met Venessa. It sometimes was weird going to the bar where they met because most everyone who works there knows Vanessa and brings her up when Matt is there. So, Matt only goes to that bar every so often. However, Matt hops around from bar to bar.

The next summer, approximately a year after the breakup, Matt takes a trip by himself to Miami Beach, Florida for 3 weeks. He stays at a high-class hotel. He goes out every night to high-end clubs and casinos. During the days Matt hangs out for hours on the beach. Some

8

days he goes to the nude beach. Matt met a woman a few times at this one club he went to quite often and invited her to after-parties in his room. Sometimes it was a girl and occasionally with 2 or 3 girls. Matt hosted 4 parties in his room during his vacation. The parties go from 4:30 AM to 10:30ish AM. Matt visited a few casinos and spent $1,200 each time he went to a casino; one time, he won $250,000 at one.

With the winnings, he rented off an entire block in South Beach and has a party going from 9 PM to 4 AM with a beach bar, a DJ, and lighting. 500 people attend, and 300 are women. The party is free but first-come-first let in due to an occupancy cap. Nudity is optional for everyone, including bartenders, and more than half of them opted to be nude by midnight. Most of the bartending staff did not at 1 AM, he asked the bartenders each if they would be willing to bartend topless for the last 3 hours of the party for $400 each, and all of them agreed.

After the party, Matt spent an hour cleaning the beach; 20 people also volunteered to stay behind and help clean too. By the time they were leaving the beach, the sun had begun to come upon the horizon. One woman who really liked Matt throughout the night said, "Hey Matt! Want some company?" As they were walking off the beach. The woman named Janette followed Matt to his hotel, and it was about 8 in the morning when they settled into the room. They stayed awake in the room until noon, drinking and watching movies, and then they both slept until 6 that evening.

After Matt and the girl woke up, they went to have fun at a casino. They visited a casino in Hollywood, FL. They got there around 9 PM and stayed there until about 3 AM. Matt spent $4,000 between gambling and drinking; this time he won nothing but had fun. When Matt and the girl returned to the hotel room, it was almost 5 that morning, and had a flight home to New York City that afternoon at 3:30. Matt and the girl got up at 1:45, Matt panicked, he woke up later than he should have. Matt got ready and pack at a quick and frantic pace, and he arrived at the airport 45 minutes before his flight left.

Getting through airport security was slow because they are short-staffed, and Matt arrived at the gate of the plane 1 minute and 5 seconds before they were going to close the door to the aircraft. When he boards the aircraft there were no seats left but a middle seat and that pisses Matt off.

Matt worked a lot when he returned home and did not go out at all for at least a month. 2 months later, he was asked by senior management to go out of town for a work trip. Matt did not really want to take this trip because he recently just took a trip. However, he accepted the offer to go anyway. The trip was to attend a 3-day investor and small business conference. The conference was in Atlanta, GA. Even though it was only a 3-day conference, he was on the trip for 5 days.

The company gave him an expense limit of $1,200 and paid for his room and his flights. On the first day when he arrived, he had about half of a day to spare, so he did some sight-seeing right away and then went to a bar that evening for a few hours. Over the next 3 days meetings started promptly at 7:30 in the morning and went till about 4 in the afternoon. Each evening after his meeting, he went to go eat and drank at a few places in the downtown Atlanta area.

On the last evening after his meetings, he hung out for a while at one bar where he met a woman. They chatted for a long while there, as Matt told her he was only there on business and leaving the next day. She was cool and down for whatever and went back to Matt's hotel room and stays with him until he leaves for the airport.

Matt gets back into New York City around 9 that night and is supposed to be at work the following day. That next day at work Matt starts his day normal as then has a meeting with company leaders. He tells them about the things he learned at the conference. Then advises new changes, the management likes everything they are hearing and thinks he has a good plan for the company.

During the following months, he works hard to help his office acquire more companies and not just small businesses anymore. Also, in his personal life, he cuts out going out for about 3 months straight. Not going out at all for 3 months saves him a lot. 4 months later, with the money he was saving, he paid off 67% of his student loan debt, which is good for only being out of school for 6 years and owing $41,000. Matt continues to work hard and gets more and more clients signed to his firm.

By the end of Matt's 4th year at his apartment and job, he could afford to move into a bigger and nicer apartment. The new studio is $800 more a month, but it is affordable for Matt. Matt is now an office general manager and scouter. In 4 years, Matt has moved way up in the company at a record pace. He also quadrupled his salary from when he started. When Matt started, he made $2,640/month and 36% commission and now is at 8,320/month and 42% commission. Matt also considered going back to school for a master's degree.

After pondering whether to go back to school or not, Matt decides to. Matt applies to attend a degree program that will be all online. After applying for 3 grants and writing 3 3000-word essays, 2 of them accept him and give $19,000, which is enough for 9 classes. Matt takes the first 9 courses within 7 months, taking 2 at a time. For the second set of 9, he paid for out of pocket. Matt finishes he is degree after 13 months, which is faster than 87% of anyone else that took this program.

After graduation, Matt got a promotion to a company executive and moved from the investment office center to corporate headquarters. Matts new office was in Time Squair in a high-rise, a bit away from the field office. He had a big office and liked his new location and position. Matt is still friends with his former co-workers, but he tells them to keep their friendship quite at work due to his high position. Matt hangs out with his old colleges at a bar almost every weekend. One night he met a girl and they quickly connected and hung out quite a lot. Matt works at his new position for a few months. While he is doing so, he is planning a trip for the following summer. It is only November as Matt begins to think about the trip, so he has some time to plan.

Ch 2: Leading Up to the Big Trip

Matt worked in his new position for about 7 months before he started to brainstorm his next personal trip. As he spent a while thinking it over, he still hung out with his friends who were old colleagues from the field office. Some were younger, and others were older, Matt's oldest friend was about 15 years older than him.

At times when everyone hangs out, some would brag about trips that have taken and for how long. Not to say, taking a vacation was a competition, but some sure made it sound like one. When they all shared stories about the trips they have taken, Matt listened more than anyone and made mental notes. Two things that his friends liked to compare are how long you went on vacation, and how much you spent.

Matt takes 6 weeks to brainstorm this new trip, and he decides that this latest trip should be a minimum of 2 months. Matt fills out a vacation request and submits it to his superior directly above him. His superior chuckles and says, "I doubt this will be approved. No one ever before in this company has been approved for this amount of vacation time. Still, I will submit it for you." As Matt walks away, his superior says, "It will be, at the very least, a month before you hear a response."

As Matt waited for his response, he just kept living his everyday life. Which consisted of working 9-6 at the corporate office and hanging out with friends every Friday and Saturday night. One night on a Friday, Matt met a nice outgoing young lady named Amanda. They then chatted for a while and played pool. At the end of the night, they shook hands and went their separate ways. Matt had no communication with her until they met approximately 2 weeks later at the same location. The second time they met, they talked a bit more. The first night they met, she told him that she had just moved to New York City earlier that week. On this night, when they left the bar, she gave him her number.

Over the next few days and weeks, Matt and Amanda talked a lot. They then started to hang out regularly too. Matt and Amanda quickly became best friends. However, it was a strictly platonic friendship, and that was established right away. Monday through Thursday, Matt never went out, but at times Amanda came over to watch movies or play video games. Matt and Amanda both liked playing video games. Even though Matt and Amanda were best friends, Matt still hung out every Friday with his other friends at the bar.

Approximately a month later, as Matt was still waiting for his vacation approval, he is asked to go on another business trip. This trip will take him to Dallas, and he will be getting a look into a business that is a massive client of his company. The trip is for 5 days, Thursday-Tuesday. The company pays for his room and flight only. His expenses are on him, which he is not pleased with because this trip is for business.

On Thursday, he arrives in Dallas at 4 PM local time, he checks into a room. After Matt is settled in, he goes to grab a bite to eat at a restaurant. He spends about an hour there and then goes to a bar where he hangs out and drinks for 3 hours. By 9:30, he gets back to his room with a 12-pack and drinks a few before going to sleep.

On Friday, he is at the company's office at 7:30 that morning. The entire morning is filled with meetings. The meeting talks about company background, growth opportunities, financing, and investing. After lunch,

19

Matt gets to shadow people as they conduct daily operations. He learns a lot and takes many notes. Towards the end of the workday, Matt sits in another meeting with executives. As everyone leaves the office, they let Matt know that on Monday, he will see more.

Matt goes back to his hotel room to rest. He dozes off and does not wake up until 9 PM. Matt then uses his phone to search for a laid-back cheap bar. He finds one, gets ready, and heads out. After an hour sitting there a woman walks in, she sits at the opposite end of the bar. Matt and this woman glance back and forth at each other for a few moments, and then she decided to move and sit in the empty seat right next to him.

When she sits down the two-start talking, and they talk for a while. Her name is Mis. Myers and she is about 38, 11 years older than Matt. She is born and raised in the area and works in a law office. Matt tells her a bit about himself and what he does for a living. Mis Myers is very impressed and says, "You're a smart one, aren't you?" Matt grins and replied, "I don't like to brag, but I guess you could say that." As the bar has is open for one more hour, Matt and Mis Myers play a game of pool.

As they leave the bar, Mis Myers says, "Your here on work, but it's the weekend. Do you want someone to hang out with and maybe a tour of the city?" Matt replies, "Yes," and then she follows Matt back to his hotel. Mis Myers sees the pool area and says, "Let's hang out there!" Matt says, "I want to drink a bit more and not trying to get in trouble with the hotel." Mis Myers says, "I know this hotel, and they are very, very laid back. Nearly anything goes with them." Matt is convinced and goes to his room to get some beers and then goes out to the pool.

The temperature is warm outside, and there is a light breeze. Matt and Mis Myers sit next to the pool with their feet in the water. They had drinks in their hands, under a bright full moon. They sit there talking for a few minutes and then Mis Myers stands up and walked to a table. She then takes off all her clothes and pops open another beer; Matt looked back as he heard a pop sound. "Wow," he says as he saw her naked from the rear. Matt turns his head back to face forward as she runs full speed doing a cannonball into the pool. Matt takes his clothes off too and gets in the pool. After 40 minutes, they get out and get half-dressed and go to Matt's room. Once in the room, they strip naked and lay in bed, as the TV is playing in the background, they have hot sex for 30 minutes and pass out right after.

The following day, they awoke around noon and get ready for the day. Miss Myers gives Matt her version of a city tour. Her tour lasts all day, and Matt saw some cool and interesting sites. Around 7 that evening, they go to the same bar they met and hang out the rest of the night there.

The next day, Sunday was a boring day where Matt spent all day in his room. Miss Myers came over to his room at about 3 that afternoon, and they just sat there watching TV and drinking. Miss Myers intended to stay until about 9 but got too drunk, so they both went to sleep.

At 7 the next morning, they both got up and went their separate ways. Matt reported to the company by 8 and spent most of the day touring and job shadowing. During lunch, Matt went to a restaurant with company leaders to discuss company operations and about a separate job office. After lunch, Matt went to a satellite office to oversee operations there. By 6 that evening, the day was done, and he went back to his room. He stayed in the room the entire night drinking and watching TV; by 11, he was asleep.

Matt flew back home to New York City, the next day, leaving Dallas at 11 in the morning. His flight made a landing to refuel in Atlanta. The pilot announced that the expected delay would be about an hour long. Matt got off the plane, grabbing in luggage from the overhead bin to go to a bar in the airport. He went to a bar near his gate and had 3 beers and 2 shots of vodka in 35 minutes, on top of the 3 beers he had before landing in Atlanta.

Matt stumbled back to the gate on time. However, he was not allowed to board due to the level of intoxication he displayed. He sat in a chair by the gate for an hour to sober up a bit and then went to a ticketing counter to see about a later flight. However, there are no more flights until the following day.

Matt finds a hotel room for the night, but it's only 7 PM so after he checks in, he goes to the hotel bar to drink for a while. As Matt hangs out, he texts his boss and uses sick pay for the next day. Matt hangs out for a little while more before going back to his room around 1 AM. Matt gets up at 9 AM the following day and is on a plane by noon back home. When Matt arrived in New York City, he went straight home and spent the day there.

Around 5, one hour after Matt got home Amanda called him and asked if he wanted to hang out. Matt said, "Sorry, but not really." "Why," Amanda asked. Matt replies, "I want to chill nude and relax," "Ok," Amanda replies. 30 minutes go by, and then Amanda says, "Fuck it, I'll come over and hang out even if I have to see your naked ass." Amanda comes over, and after 20 minutes, she says, "Know what, why not." Taking off her shoes, socks, shirt, pants, bra, underwear. They continue to hang out and play video games until 11 that night, then Amanda left, and Matt went to sleep.

The next day, Thursday, Matt went to work and spent most of the day in meetings discussing what he observed on the trip. After work, he hung out with some friends. They went to a bar-based arcade that had recently opened. Throughout the following months, Matt worked almost every day and did not go out anywhere except once every other week.

However, he did hang out with Amanda a lot. He also talked on the phone and through video calls with Miss Myers.

One month after Matt returned home from the business trip and 2 months after he put in for his vacation, his 2-month vacation was approved. So now it was time for him to plan it out.

As he spent time planning his trip he talked with his friends about it. Since he has a 2 month, he wanted to plan out at least 3 destinations. Matt remembers that one of his friends talk about their grand vacation, Matt wanted to top that and have a more extravagant one.

As Matt was planning his trip and hanging out with Amanda, she expressed interest in wanting to go. She said that she could cover her own expenses and plane tickets, but not hotel rooms. Matt asked, "Would you have a problem sharing a hotel rooms with me?" "No," she replied. Then Matt asked, "What about seeing me naked?" she again replies, "No." Matt tells her to request 2 months off or at least a month, she responds by saying, "I'll see what I can do."

Three weeks after that conversation and 5 weeks brainstorming his trip, he has a plan. Take a bus from New York City to Atlantic City, and spend 5 days there, then fly to San Francisco and spend 6 days there, then take a train from San Franco to Los Angeles and spend 20 days there.

After his time in California, he would take a bus to Las Vegas, where he would spend 4 days. He would fly to Miami, going to the Florida Keys and spending 6 days there and then 8 days back in Miami. Matt's travel and room charges would be about $18,000, and his planned expenses would be $14,500. However, he factored in another $4,000 just in case.

A month before Matt's vacation would begin, he hung out with his friends once at a bar and once had a gathering at his place. He also spent a lot of time with Amanda, and she was going on his trip with him for the first month. Matt was also keeping in contact with Miss Myres, just to be friendly. One night, about 10 days before the trip, Miss Myers showed up in a bar in New York City where Matt was. They talked and had fun. They got really drunk and at the end of the night, Miss Myres went back with Matt to his apartment.

The next morning, when they both get up, they sit in the living room. Miss Myres said, "Last night was amazing." "It was." Said Matt. Mis Myers, after a few moments of silence, procreated to tell Matt that she really likes him and wants more, she just took a new job in New York City to be with him. Matt is beyond shocked, and he takes a few moments to respond. When he responds, he uses carefully chosen words. To tell her that there is no mutual feeling and reminds her that they agreed to keep it casual. Miss Myres then leaves Matt's apartment without a single word. Matt feels terrible and texts and calls after a few hours and gets no response.

Matt sits at home for a few hours thinking about his relationship with Miss Myres. He does not believe he led Miss Myers on but, feels terrible. After about an hour doing nothing, Matt began packing up. Matt took a break from packing at around 5 to go grab food and drinks and then returns to his apartment roughly an hour later.

Amanda came over that night and could tell something was wrong, so she asked Matt "What's wrong?" So, Matt explained everything to Amanda. "As it sounds to me, I don't think you did anything wrong. If she thought differently, that's out of your control, don't worry." Amanda tells him. Matt thanks her and feels better. Matt and Amanda then hang out that night talking mostly about the trip.

Ch. 3: The First Half of the Big Trip

On Monday, May 27th, Matt was at a bar with his friends and Amanda and hanging out. They all knew that he was leaving in 7 days for his trip, so this was like a sendoff party. After Monday night, Matt worked the rest of the week, and Friday would be the last day in the office. On Friday night, he just drank at home alone as he started packing his luggage. Amanda came over the next day, with her bags, and spent the night with Matt Saturday and Sunday night. As they were at Matt's place for 2 days, they hung out nude quite a lot.

Monday, June 3rd, Matt and Amanda got up around 9 in the morning and left an hour later. They took a taxi to the bus station and boarded a bus to Atlantic City at 11:15. It departed at 11:25, the bus ride was about an hour and 15 minutes and had no additional stops.

In Atlantic City, they took a taxi from the transit station to their hotel 3.6 miles away. They made a pit stop at a liquor store before getting to the hotel. By 2:45, they arrived at the hotel, which was a luxurious hotel and casino. Matt and Amanda were staying in a suite on the top floor. They were delighted with the hotel and with the fact that the pool area and fitness center were always open for use.

After getting into the room, Matt and Amanda decided to hang out there for a while, drinking the beverages they got along the way. Though pricey, they opted to order food to there room from room service. After having a few drinks in them, they decided to pack a few more.

Then they decided to go look at the fitness center. The fitness center was open but empty, it was like almost midnight. Matt got on some of the equipment, and Amanda did some yoga. After 25 minutes, Matt takes a rest for 10, and it is still just the two of them. Matt notices that the windows are very tinted and that there are no security cameras and asks Amanda, "Want to work out naked?" "Hell yeah," she replies, and then they continue to work out for 15 minutes. They then go to the pool area, with nothing on, through a door on the other end of the fitness center.

As soon as they walk through the door, they see other people and say, "O shit!" and walk back through the door to get clothes on. Before they get dressed, a topless woman in her mid-40's walks in and says, "What the fuck are y'all thinking?" Everyone is in silence, then she proceeds to say, "Just messing with y'all. Nudity is ok in the hotel; except in the casino. I learned that my second day here." Matt and Amanda feel much better and head to the pool area. There were about 20 people there, and most of them were naked when

Matt and Amanda got tired, they walked with no cloths on back to their room and fell asleep instantly

They get up around 3 in the afternoon and go into the casino area and play. They play roulette and win $3000 after paying $350 over 2 hours. After they win, they go to other casinos on the strip. There they eat first and then played later. They ate at an Italian restaurant and then Matt played poker for a while. Amanda sat there and watched. Matt bought in for $1800 and lost it all, then as Amanda is screaming no, he buys in again for $1600, he plays for 1 hour and walks away with $2200. After that, they go back to the room where they spend the rest of the night.

The next day, they tour the city, which is nothing worth seeing. By noon they are done touring and spend some time at a casino; they spend about 6 hours at one spending $1500 but winning $4500. They are shocked by how much they won.

They then go to a liquor store to buy a lot to drink before going to the hotel. At the hotel, they immediately go to the fitness center and get naked. They start to work out, and after 5 minutes, more people walk in. Amanda shouts, "Get naked, get $100 bucks!!!" most inquire about this offer and accept. Amanda explains, "If you get naked and are ok with us working out naked, everyone will get $100 each from us." Of the 25 people there working out, 22 of them accepted, and most went into the pool area to relax after their workout.

By 3 the following morning, Matt and Amanda went up to their room. They watched TV for an hour then went to sleep. Their next day, was their last full day in Atlantic City, they spent most of the day doing city tours and learning about the history of Atlantic City. In the mid-evening, they went to a rooftop restaurant where they ate a big dinner and took in the amazing skyline view. After dinner, they decided to not do much for the rest of the night. So, on their way back to their hotel room, they stopped at a liquor store then went straight to their room.

They hung out that night, just the two of them getting drunk in their room. After like 2 hours and them being naked for half of it, Amanda asked, "If we were to have sex, would you be confused or want a relationship?" Matt replies, "No, and I don't feel like it would hurt our friendship. Why do you want to have sex?" "Well…. I mean sort of, it's been a good minute for me." Amanda says. Amanda gets herself aroused and gets Matt aroused, too, then they proceed to have sex. Afterword's Matt takes a bath to get ready for bed while Amanda is thinking to herself, "I liked that. It will happen again." After Matt gets out of the shower, they both go to sleep. They get up at 8 the next morning leaving the hotel by 9:15 within 30 minutes they arrive at their airport 2 hours before their departure.

The ticket counter and security line are extremely busy. It takes them an hour and 15 minutes to get through to the airside. Matt says, "It has never taken me this long before to get to the gate… wow…" once getting near the gate they go get a few drinks at a bar. Within 35 minutes before there scheduled departure, they go to the gate. However, when they get there, they see that their flight is delayed an hour behind schedule due to inclement weather.

Matt and Amanda then go back to the bar they just at and get 2 more drinks. They then go back to their gate to board their plane. They have a long 7-hour flight but are comfortable as they are seated in first class and drinking throughout most of the flight. They arrived in San Francisco at approximately 7 PM local time. After arrival, they are so exhausted that they just go to their hotel and relax there the entire night. The hotel is on the bay, and their room is a suite with a beautiful skyline view.

The next day, their first full day in San Francisco, they get up early and do some sightseeing and tours. They had a city go card, so on their first day they go visit 3 attractions and do one tour, the Go City Card has 12 attractions and 6 tours they can do over a week. That evening they find a chill pub to go to drank at. Close to midnight, the pool area at their hotel was open and empty. They spend an hour swimming in their underwear then get into the hot tub removing their underwear as nobody has been around. They hang in the hot tub for about 25 minutes and call it a night.

The following day they have a late start and get up around 2 in the afternoon. They do one attraction, which takes the rest day, then by 8 that evening they have dinner and go out drinking at a pub. A couple hours later, they are exhausted, so they return to their room where they rest for the night.

On the next day, they get up right after dawn and eat a big breakfast. Then throughout the day, go on 2 tours, for 2 hours each, and they do one attraction. By 7, they head back to their room, grabbing a bite on the way. They chill out and watch TV, and by 10 PM, they are both asleep.

At about 9 the following morning, they get up and get ready. By 10:15, Matt and Amanda get an Uber to their first attraction. They spend close to an hour and a half there, then after they do one tour lasting an hour and another attraction after that. They then go get dinner and then head back to the hotel. After they rest for a few hours, they go to a bar a few miles away, spending the rest of the night there at the bar. They leave the bar 15 minutes before the alcohol cut-off time to go to a liquor store and buy more drinks.

Then they head to a beach area right behind their hotel. As its 3 in the morning, they go to the beach, take off all their clothes and start drinking more. 20 minutes later, a few people are in their view, in a frantic Matt and Amanda cover up a bit. However, 2 young couples around them sit down only about 150 feet away. After 5 minutes in this situation, they do not care and uncover and party on. The other 2 couples then get naked as well and drank, still 150 feet away. Then one couple goes to Matt and Amanda and says, "We should combine parties." They agree and move their things closer together. At dawn, as the sun hits the horizon, everyone `gets dressed and goes back to their hotel rooms.

Matt and Amanda stay up until about 10, drinking and watching TV, they then fall asleep and sleep the entire day until 8 that night. They order room service for dinner and stay up watching TV until 1 then falls back asleep.

The following morning, they wake up and plan to visit a national park just 35 minutes outside of san Francisco. There drive to the park was nice and scenic as they drive on the Golden Gate Bridge. Around noon they arrive at the park and spend a good amount of the day there. They pay to rent a golf cart, so they do not have to walk, and the attendant says, "You picked a good day because no one else is here yet." It was a weekday.

They drive the first 10 minutes in, and with no one around, Amanda decided to take off her top, shirt, and bra, matt took his shirt off too. Then they drive off the trail into the woods, and they drive 30 minutes. The park near a lake; both take off their bottoms and go for a dip. They then set up a blanket to sit on as they eat and drink. They sit there and chill as they are naked for about 3 hours. Then they get back on the golf cart and drive a little deeper into the woods. At their turn-around point, they have a 40-minute drive out of the woods and back to the main trail. They drive 40 minutes back to the path and get dressed as they reach the trail.

When they leave the park, they go to a casino 30 minutes away and 75 minutes form their hotel. It is about 8 when they get to the casino. Matt sits at a blackjack table and buys in for $350. He plays for about 2 hours and walks away with $975. Then Matt and Amanda go to a bar in the casino where they drank and chat, they spend $225 at the bar, and by 3 AM they get a uber back to their hotel.

The uber ride is about 75 minutes, and Amanda asks, as she is in the back seat. "Do you mind if I take my top off? I've always wanted to be riding in a car topless." The driver replies, "Wow! I don't know what to think or say." Matt then gives the driver $250 in cash, and then the driver says, "Ok, you too do whatever you want;

just be ready to get out at your stop. Amanda then takes off her top, and 20 minutes later, Matt pulls down his pants. Amanda gives matt a hand job, and then they both get dressed as they are 10 minutes from the hotel.

They get to the hotel at around 4:45 and immediately take off their clothes as they get into their room. They then have sex, which is only like the 3rd time they have done it together. It lasts for about 30 minutes, then they both go to sleep. They do not wake up until late in the afternoon the next day, which is their last full day in San Francisco. Around 7, they go out to a nice dinner where they apparently spend an hour and a half, then they go to a bar. They hang out, drank, play pool, and chat with other people for a while. They have fun and meet some cool people; they leave right after the last call is announced. They arrived back at their hotel a bit later then they wanted to, so when Matt and Amanda got in their room, they went right to sleep.

The following morning, Matt and Amanda they get up mid-morning like just before 10, they leave the hotel within an hour and go to the train station. Their train is scheduled to leave at 12:45, and they get there with 35 minutes to spare. Their train ride from San Francisco to Los Angeles will take about 5 and a half hours. They spend most of their ride in the dining car, where they play cards at a table and drank a lot. In fact, they spend $75 on the train.

They arrive in Los Angeles at around 7 that evening. For their full 20 days, they stay at a hotel closes to all trains for $4675. After they get settled into their room, they go to a bar one block over from the hotel and hand out until closing time. The following day they get up around 11 and leave their hotel about an hour later. They go to a studio tour at Sony, it lasted almost 2 hours. Then they go walk along Venice Beach until right after sunset. Then about 40 minutes after sunset, they made their way to a bar a half a block from the Venice Beach boardwalk and chilled there for a few hours.

Their second day in Los Angeles, they spent the day in Hollywood. Where they did 4 tours. Two of the tours were touring theaters and lasted 30 minutes each. The other tours were riding around Hollywood for 2 hours each. That evening Matt and Amanda spent a few hours checking out a few bars before getting the train back to their hotel. At the hotel, they had a stash of drinks and decided to go check out the pool. It was open surprisingly at 1 AM, so they chilled there for a few hours.

Matt and Amanda did not go to bed until the morning hours. They slept for a short time, getting up in the mid-afternoon. They then decided to go see Santa Monica, and they got there with a couple hours of daylight left. They stayed on the beach for a few hours. After watching a nice sunset and relaxing on the beach, they take a stroll on the famous 3RD St. Premade. They did some shopping, dining, and drinking before getting back on the train to their hotel in Downtown Los Angeles. After they got off the 40-minute train ride, they found a bar close to their hotel and decided to hang out there for an hour. They left after an hour but like the atmosphere and the vibe so they would sourly visit again very soon.

They woke up mid-morning the following day and went to a theme park. To get there, they just took one train for a 26-minute ride. They got to the park around noon and spent a few hours there, they both had a blast. After they left the park, they looked at a few shops and went to a restaurant on a strip right next to the park. Near midnight they boarded a train and took it back to Downtown. They went back to the bar a few blocks and stayed there

for about an hour before heading back to their hotel.

The morning after they woke up mid-morning. Matt and Amada ordered breakfast from room service and hung out in their room for a bit. They then went to a TV game show about 1 PM and were in the running to be contestants, Amanda did get selected and won like $4500. When they left the show, they went out to celebrate, and Amanda, being the good friend that she is, paid for everything. They went back to their hotel to party at 10 PM. Amanda had 3 other girls come over.

As they are all in the room drinking and having a good time, Amanda whispers to the 3 girls, "One at a time go into the bathroom, strip naked and walk out." So, one did, and Matt was like, what are you doing. Then 6 minutes another girl did, and Matt said well I like this, as he sat casually on the bed. Then Amanda went to the bathroom, took off her clothes, and came out. Matt then started to undress and said party on. The last girl than did the same then.

They all hung out totally nude and partied until almost daybreak. During their party, porn was on the TV, they were playing cards, an orgy and some illegal drug use took place along with heavy drinking. When the parting was done, everyone slept in the one bed in the room, resting for 16 hours in a row. They all woke up the following evening and did nothing.

The day after, when Matt and Amanda were well-rested, they spent the day doing another 2 tours, lasting an hour and a half each, and visited one attraction. That night they did not do much. They only had 4 more days left in the Los Angeles area, but they were not quite sure of anything else to do.

After hours online, Matt found a nudist and swingers resort about 80 minutes from Los Angeles. Matt showed Amanda, and they discussed it. After talking it over for at least 2 hours, they decided to go for 2 of their last 3 days. They called right away and made the reservation for the following two nights. They got up the following morning around 10 and left their hotel in Los Angeles about an hour later.

When they got to the resort, their room was not ready because it was early, but their bags were stored, and they were shown around the resort. They got dropped off at a hangout spot after the tour, where clothes immediately started to come off. After a while of it being just them two, another couple came in the area being completely naked. The other couple then went over to the beds. They right away started playing, Matt and Amanda then got another bed and started playing too. It lasted for about 30 minutes, and then the 4 of them went into the outdoor hot tub.

In the mid-evening, Matt and Amanda went back to their room to eat and relax. The walk was about 1200-feet, and even though they had their clothes with them, they chose not to put them back on. They spent approximately 2 hours in their room then took drinks with them to the clubhouse. They left their room wearing nothing but shoes. They spent several hours in the clubhouse, and for the first couple of hours, they were alone. In their first hour, they played 2 games of pool, and there second hour, they spent some time in the indoor hot tub. A few other couples started strolling in after that, and all of them were naked. Matt and Amanda were not shy and got out of the hot tub and mingled with all of them.

There was a playroom with beds in the clubhouse, and after a couple hours of drinking, everyone went there. Amanda started playing with Matt, then a few minutes later, Amanda played with someone else while Matt did the same. Everyone hung out playing and watching one another for about an hour than most called it a night. However, Matt, Amanda, and one couple stayed in the clubhouse for a few more hours drinking. By about 3 in the morning, they call it a night.

The next day Matt and Amanda get up mid-afternoon and walk the trail up a big hill and into some woods. They both enjoyed seeing and exploring wooded nature trails. The hike too them a few hours, so when they got back, they took a quick dip in the pool and then went to their room. They both dozed off, but Matt only slept a couple hours. Matt then went by himself to the outdoor hot tub. Another couple was in the hot tub too, but they did not mind. He sat in the hot tub, drinking for about 30 minutes, and the couple got out after about 10 minutes. Matt then walked back to the room.

Amanda was still sleeping, so he got more drinks and then goes to the clubhouse, it would empty and late. Matt gets into the hot tub, and then a girl shows up, and she is totally naked. She gets in with Matt, and they talk. The more they are discussing, the closer they get to each other. They eventually start touching each other, and it escalates to more.

The following day they leave the resort right before noon and return to Los Angeles where their bus will depart the next day. Once they return to their downtown hotel, they do not do anything for the rest of the day. Amanda and Matt are both pretty much existed, and they need to save money for the 4 day's they will be in Vegas. There last afternoon and night in Los Angeles is spent drinking and relaxing in their room.

Amanda's vacation is in the final days, and she will have to go back home. However, after Vegas, Matt is going to South Florida, he thinks, for 3 and a half weeks. Matt and Amanda both pass out around midnight. The next day they get up, get ready, and catch their bus to Las Vegas at around noon. They get to their hotel on the Vegas strip at just before 6

PM. They both nap for a few hours until about 11 PM and then go play and drank in the casino of their hotel until 3:45 AM.

The next day they get up mid-morning and go on a bus tour to the Grand Canyon. They get to the canyon with 25n other people, and they have 2 hours before the bus departs back. Matt and Amanda walk around with 4 others and tour the canyon. They then get back to the Vegas strip at about 7 and go casino hopping for hours. 2 of the 4 people that Matt and Amanda toured the canyon with casino hop with them. The 4 of them stay out until 3 AM, and then Matt and Amanda invite them back to their hotel. At the hotel, they ask if they can have private access to the pool until 9 AM. The manager says, "Not really allowed, but how much are you willing to pay?" Matt then hands a stack of cash to them, totaling $3,800. The manager speaks and sneaks them a key and says, "I'll shut off the cameras for that area and don't return this key until you personally see me."

Matt and Amanda then go up to their room to get more drinks, and the couple follows them. They grab a cooler and fill it up and then grab towels too, then they head to the pool area. They then start drinking, and then the couple asks, "How are we going to get in the pool and hot tub we don't have bathing suits?" Amanda replies, "Naked" and starts taking off her clothes. The couple then walks away for a minute, and then they come back and just smile as they take their clothes off too. They then drink for a few more minutes before they all get in the pool. They spend about 45 minutes swimming, then they get out and sit around a table for 25 minutes drinking. As they are sitting there drinking, they have their towels on the chairs they are sitting in, and no one is covering up. They then go into the hot tub and sit in there with drinks. After an hour, by 8:15 AM, Amanda and Matt go to their room. While the couple retreat to their hotel down the street.

Matt and Amanda spend most of that day sleeping and stay in bed until 9 that night. Matt wants to go play, but Amanda wants to rest because she is going back home the next day. So, Matt goes alone to go play in the casino at the hotel he is staying at. Matt spends 6 hours playing and spends $4,200 playing roulette. At first, he loses $1,600, but then he goes on a winning streak and walks away with $8,200. Matt then plays table games for 2 hours. By the time he goes back to his hotel, his $4,200 is 9,050.

The next morning Matt and Amanda both get up around 9, and Amanda must quickly get ready and say goodbye. She leaves the room at 10:15 and goes to the airport for her flight at 12 noon. Meanwhile, Matt checks out of the room and hangs out in the casino until 2. He drinks and plays a bit, spending $1,250 but then walking out with $1,600. Then makes his 4:10 flight, his flight gets delayed, and they do not begin boarding until 4:17. So with 45 minutes, he goes to drank 2 beers at a bar near the gate. The plane takes off at 4:36.

Ch. 4: The Big Trip Part ll- The First 3 Weeks on the Island

As they are in the air, Matt is enjoying the flight with a cold beer in his hands. An hour into them flying at cruising altitude, they are told by the flight crew that the plane has started to have mechanical issues and had to do an emergency stop. As they descend from cruising altitude they see a weird shaped small island, that none of them have known about before and land on it. This island is in the center of the Gulf of Mexico. Ten minutes after they land, the pilot asks everyone to exit and tells everyone a new plane will be here in approximately 6 hours. All checked bags will be laid out, and when the next plane comes, they must be claimed before putting them back on the aircraft. The plane landed on a grassy strip of land, that was nearly a mile and a half away from any water.

After Matt hears that, he takes his bags and puts them by a tree out of sight from others. Then, being the adventurist that he is. Matt takes some time wondering the island just to explore this newly discovered island. Matt has always been an adventurist even when he was a young boy. Until Matt was about eleven, he and his parents traveled all over the world. They mostly stayed in the states, but there were a couple of places they lived abroad.

Losing track of time, Matt goes slightly deep into the center of the island. A 17-year-old girl, wearing a tank top and jean pants, named Moreen follows close behind him, without him knowing. Moreen is a petite black young girl with an outgoing and enthusiastic personality. She is nicely endowed with excellent physical features, like beautiful perfect breasts. She has a good head on her shoulders as she was going to college to be a teacher.

Moreen had a rough life growing up in foster care from age 10 to 18. She had opportunities to be adopted, especially in her mid-teenage years, but declined each time, so that she could do whatever she wanted when she turned into an adult. In school, she made great grates and did well on her college exams. For her 4 years in high school, she played basketball and was on her way to attend a University in South Florida to play for them.

Moreen is traveling alone, leaving where she grew up, Nevada, and going to South Florida. Moreen has a government ID and should be considered as an independent adult, due to the fact, that she is 17 for about a week longer. She got her ID a couple weeks before her flight because she was aging out of the foster care system of Nevada to go off to college.

Matt has walked deep into the middle of the island and finds himself standing in a grassy field. The grass is very green and a ton of trees are surrounding him. As he stands there, there is a light breeze that soothes the heat from the bright sun. As Matt walks around the field, he turns around and seas Moreen. He did not notice Moreen until he turns around to take in the scenery after walking close to 2 and a half hours. "Hi, I'm Matt, who are you?" Matt says.

Moreen responded, "I'm Moreen, sorry I wanted to explore too. Cool island." "Yes, it is, but we should head back soon, so we don't miss the plane," Matt replies.

They spend a few minutes resting before slowly walking back, taking in the scene of this undiscovered island. During their way back to get on the new plane, they hear another plane as they are still a few miles away and start running, but they get back too late. As the doors of the plane shut, they try to wave at the people on board. However. No one sees them, and it takes off right in front of them. They both stand there looking at each other. Matt puts his arms in the air and yells "What the Fuck!" Then they both stand there in silence for a bit looking at one another.

Matt and Moreen are now stuck on this island with all their luggage from the plane. With the old plane left sitting there. Matt believes he has a few hours of daylight left, so he looks around the island in search of any type of shelter, there is none. They now must spend this night trying to sleep in the old plane, but there is no ladder to get up into one of the doors. However, Matt finds two very long pieces of tree trunks and creates a ramp for them to walk up into the plane.

The ramp took about 35 minutes to be Installed into a good enough position to climb up. However, walking up the slope was still challenging for them at first. After getting inside the plane, they got as comfortable as they could. Matt sleeps in the back section of the aircraft, and Moreen sleeps a few rows in front of him. Matt lays there for hours but cannot rest, so as Moreen is sound asleep, Matt gets up and walks off the plane.

With the moon shining brightly and using his phone's flashlight, he walks about a half a mile to the nearest part of the island that the ocean is on. Matt then removes all his clothes and gets in the water. After spending some time in the water, he goes up to the sand and sits there still in shock, that he is stuck on this island. He then lays on the sand for a moment to enjoy the light breeze on his naked body, but soon after he lays down, he dozes off for a few hours.

Matt wakes up just after sunrise and gets dressed and walks back to the plane, which is close to a mile and a half away. As he arrives, Moreen is still in the plane sound asleep, as matt is hungry, he looks throughout the plane to see if any food was left behind. There luckily was some snack size bags of cookies and chips and a few sodas. He eats some chips and has one drink.

Matt then walks back off the plane and sat outside in the grass under the wing of the plane. Moreen then awakes hours later and looks out the window. She then looks towards the back of the plane and says, "Matt... Matt, you awake. Matt?" "Outside!" Matt yells in response. Moreen looks out the door as she stands in the doorway, "I don't see you." "I'm sitting under the wing!" Matt shouts. Moreen then says, "Ok." As she goes back inside, she does what Matt did and looks for food.

At around noon Matt and Moreen both go out to the beach. That they can see through the trees next to where the plane is. Once at the beach, they sit down on the sand and chill out watching the waves. "If we could get that plane a little closer to this spot, it is better for us," Moreen says. "I agree, but not possible. However, if we are not rescued in a few days, I will build a shelter here on the beach.

They decide to go for a dip in the water but are not wearing swimsuits. So, they both strip down to their underwear and go for a swim in the ocean for a bit. After swimming, they sit on the shoreline for a bit, enjoying the waves smashing up on them. They sit there until after sunset and then walk back to the plane and dose off. Matt wakes up a couple hours later, and with it being so uncomfortable sleeping in the plane, he spends a few hours during the middle of the night constructing a shelter outside.

With the moon well lighting the island, he first goes around and collects tree trunks and twigs. When he has enough peaces piled up, he starts building. However, before he starts, he strips down butt naked as it is hot and he is drenched in sweat. The roof of the shelter goes up first, and its 2 tree trunks stretched between to trees 8 feet in length apart. He hooks them into tree branches that are 5 and a half feet high. As he is working on building the roof Moreen awakes and comes outside, Matt works for a minute and turns around. "You're up! Oops, sorry about this." Matt says and starts to put clothes on. "I'm up, yes, and it's fine. If you want to be naked, it's totally cool." Moreen says. "Ok," Matt says and stays naked and turns around to continue building it.

Matt knew about shelter building and survival skills because his pop taught him about it at a very young age when the two of them went camping. Camping was there bonding time as Matt's father was a busy man as he served in the Army and was always on missions that kept him away from home a lot.

As it is still the middle of the night, Moreen walks to the ocean, removes all her clothes, and gets in for a while. Just before the sun starts to rise, Moreen walks back to the site and sees the little shelter built and Matt laying there sleeping under it. She then lays down next to him without putting on a top.

Around noon Matt and Moreen both wake-up; Matt is shocked that she is topless. Matt then goes to his luggage, pulls out some shorts, and puts them on. Then Moreen changes her bottoms but says, "I'm comfortable, so I'm not going to be wearing a top today." Then they go on the plane to get some snacks and go eat outside. After an hour, Matt thought of a way to make a fishing rod and it takes him an hour to make it, and then they go test it out. They then walk out to the beach to chill out and for Matt to go spearfishing. But before they enter the water, they both decide to remove all their clothing.

As Moreen swims around in the water, Matt fishes for their dinner. After about an hour and a half, Matt collects 4 big fishes and then relaxes and swims around with Moreen until the sun begins setting. As the sun is setting on the horizon, they exit the water. Up on the beach, they collect their clothing and the fish. Then walk back to the site where all their belongings are. Matt starts a fire, and then once it started, Matt prepares to cook the fish for them. They then eat and sit there for a while. Before laying down, they both put some bottoms on and went under the newly made shelter.

Matt and Moreen laid down to get some sleep. As they were lying in the shelter that Matt just made. Soon after they laid down it started raining, and it continued for about 80 minutes. The rain came down hard at some periods. When it stopped, they both had to change clothes as they both were soaked. As they both were changing in the dark, they both decided to just sleep in underwear. They laid back down. With them both wearing only underwear and fell asleep. However, Moreen laid down last and chose to wear nothing at all.

By 8 the next morning, Matt wakes up, as Moreen is still sound asleep. He does not wake up but looks at her as she is laying there totally naked and looking cute. Matt gets some shorts on, and then Matt spends hours hunting for food. He finds some and drops it off by their campsite. Moreen is still asleep, Matt then goes to bathe in the water. He undresses at the shelter and walks a mile and a half to the ocean, after washing himself he puts a towel around him.

He goes back to the campsite, puts on a clean pair of shorts, and starts a fire to cook. Moreen wakes up and starts getting dress but opts not to wear any top, as its way too hot. By 3 that afternoon, Matt and Moreen take a walk around the island. One of them goes one way, and the other goes the opposite. It is sweltering outside, so after Moreen leaves, Matt strips down naked and then goes for a walk. The wind and everything feels good on Matt's naked body.

He finds a nice clear sandy area near the water and thinks about building a new shelter. Matt finds 4 big trees, almost evenly spread out, and they are only 200 feet from the ocean. The time to build shelter takes him like 4 hours, and Matt can build the shelter using different things from the first one, and the new objects would make for a better shelter. As he is building it, Moreen shows up. Matt is scared and says, "Sorry, I'm naked, again, but it was just way too hot." Moreen replies, "I already told you the other day, not a big deal," as she is not wearing a top. Moreen asks, "Would you like me to start moving our stuff over here?" "If you want, yes, go ahead," Matt says. Before Moreen starts, she takes off her bottoms to be totally naked because she is hot too.

It takes Moreen 4 trips to bring everything over, and when she is done, she goes in the water for a while. Matt joins her in the water about an hour later after the shelter is built. As Matt is in the water, he tries to catch fish with a net basket he made. When they both get out of the water, they both put on only shorts. Moreen, yet again, does not put on a top and finds it comfortable to have her bare breasts out. They manage to catch some fish, and they exit the water. At around sunset, Matt starts a fire, he then cooks the fish, and they eat it. As the sun sets, they hang by the fire for a bit, and as they get tired, Matt puts out the fire, and they both go to sleep.

They both wake up a few hours later as they are having trouble sleeping. Matt starts a fire so they can see and then he walks with a blanket down near the water, then he removes his shorts and attempts to please himself. Moreen walks over in the middle of Matt doing it, and she then takes off her shorts. Moreen then grabs Matts dick and plays with it before performing oral. She stops after several minutes, and Matt finishes himself off. They then both attempt to get a few more hours of rest.

Matt dozes off but only for like an hour, and Moreen sleeps for a few hours. Shortly after daybreak Matt hears a plane, he tries to signal it, but Fales and they are now about to spend their second full day on this island alone. Matt begins to look around the island for sticks and stuff to make hunting tools with. Matt is still naked as he is walking around the island. Matt gathers a lot of things and brings it back to the campsite. Moreen is just waking up as Matt returns. Moreen then goes to walk around by herself, but before she does, she puts on some shorts.

Moreen walks around for a few hours, and when she arrives back at the campsite, Matt is in the water fishing. Matt catches 5 fish and cooks 2 of them that night. As Matt is cooking, he has shorts on. They eat during sunset, and then a rain shower comes through.

The rain comes down hard and lasts for a half-hour, as it is raining, they are in the shelter but still getting wet because the roof is made of tree ends. So, because they are getting wet from the rain, they both go ahead and lose their bottoms. They then lay back down in the shelter. As they lay their butt naked, Matt gets hard and Moreen notices. Moreen starts preforming oral, and minutes later, she climbs on top of Matt, who is lying on his back, and puts his hard cock inside of her. They have sex for a few moments as the rain is coming down on them hard, and then Moreen jumps off if his cock right before his load shoots out. They then cuddle up and go to sleep.

The next day Matt searches for wood and find some to put on top of the tree greens covering the roof of their shelter. Matt and Moreen spend most of the day with little to no clothing on because of how hot it is. After walking around collecting wood the entire day, Matt and Moreen go for a dip in the water for a bit. As the sun is slowly creeping away, they exit the water and go up to the campsite.

Matt is missing beer to drink, and he says so out loud, just because. Moreen follows suit and says out loud what she missies. Then Matt and Moreen sit there by the campsite with a fire going, eating and talking to each other about themselves and what they miss. They share what their favorite foods and beverages are as well as some things that they enjoy doing in their free time. Moreen does not reveal her age as she is turning 18 any day, her birthday was 4 days after the flight they were on.

Matt and Moreen have been on the

island for 3 days and 14 hours, and it is now 1AM on day 4, a genie appears and wakes them up. They both wake up in shock as they are laying there in underwear. The genie says, "Ask me anything you want, but you can't get off the island." They ask for unlimited food and alcohol and extra tree wood. The genie replies, "Will be granted if you burn all your clothing, including what you are currently wearing." They look at each other and nod in agreement.

Matt and Moreen first burn everything in their suitcases then Moreen looks around before she takes off her panties that she has on and throws it into the fire, then Matt removes his underwear. The genie then says, "Nothing can be used to cover any body parts for the next 39 hours even when sleeping." They then lay back down and try to fall back asleep, but for both, it was hard. So, with it being 2 AM, they just stayed up. Within an hour, a massive amount of food and drinks, including alcohol, appeared near their shelter. Matt was excited to have a beer again for the first time in 4 days.

They feasted on the food around the fire, and Matt started drinking a lot. At sunrise, they both decided to go on a hike together. They hike for about a few hours, through a shallow forest to a beach. The beach to the southernmost point of the island, which was 4 and a half miles. Then when they stop, they hang out in the water for an hour before walking back to their site via the beach.

As the sun is beginning to set, Matt makes a fire, and he and Moreen sit by the fire for some hours eating and drinking. Moreen says, "I never tried beer, can I?" Matt: assuming that she is about 22 says, "Of course." It then starts to rain, but they do not care and go sit down by the water to glaze at the bright moon and the night sky. The rain brings a gentle light breeze along with it, and it cools the temperature a bit.

After a long day and pleasant evening, they make their way back under the shelter and lay down. As they lay there for a few moments separately, they are not comfortable, so then start to cuddle Moreens back is on Matt's chest, and Moreen can feel Matts private in the small of her back. Matt puts his arm around Moreen and, with his hand, cups her breasts. They both dose off into a deep sleep in that position. The next morning, they wake up around sunrise. Matt gets embarrassed as he has morning wood and Moreen felt the stiffness. Without saying a word, Moreen grabs it with her hand and guides it inside of her

Matt and Moreen are both laying on their side, as Matt's dick is inside of her. He is barely thrusting here at first, so his dick is just sitting inside of her pussy, and Matt's hand is still cupping her boob, but as they become more awake, he gets more into it. Matt rolls on his back, and Moreen gets on top of him and puts it back in. After 15 minutes, Matt finishes inside of her and then they both go down to bathe in the water. As they wash themselves, Moreen says, "That felt really good, can we do that a few times a day?" Matt smiles and says, "Yes, of course!" as they walk back up to the shelter, they hold hands.

They then sit in the shelter and eat for a bit. With it still being early, they lay back down after the eat and have more intercourse. When they finish, they lay there for an hour. When they finally get up, they decide to go for a hike together around the island. About 20 minutes into their hike they hear thunder, Matt then runs to look on the beach and up at the sky. "O Man," he says as it looks like a very bad storm is approaching. He goes back by Moreen and says, "quickly; back to the shelter!" as they run back, it starts to lightly rain, but then it begins to pour. Luckily, by the time it is pouring, they are within 1000- feet from the shelter. They get in the shelter as it is raining hard, thundering, and lighting.

As they sit there in this storm, they begin to look at each outer and Moreen pushes Matt down to lay on his back. With them, both already naked, she gets on top of him and puts his man part inside of her. As they are having intercourse, the wind picks up, and they experience 25mph winds. The roof of the shelter gets destroyed, but as it does, they do not stop. After Moreen rides Matt for a bit, she gets on all fours, and Matt boned her from behind. They finish together as they are spooning and with Matt's cock inside of her. They then lay there for a little while longer, and after 25 minutes, the storm is still going strong. With the storm being just heavy wind and rain, they walk down to the beach and sit in the water. The waves are enormous, but they sit in a position where they would not get pulled out to sea.

After 45 minutes, the storm starts to calm down, and the mid-afternoon sun attempts to arise from behind the clouds. As the sun comes out, Matt rebuilds a roof for the shelter. He finds heavier bamboo then he had before and more bamboo shams. As he is rebuilding, Moreen is having fun looking at him and his "" You know what"" swing and hanging and it turns her on. So, sexually influences Matt to take a break by lying on the ground right near him and spreads her legs and begins touching herself. As Matt sees it, he tries to ignore it, but his dick is not and gets hard. As he attempts to keep working on the shelter, Moreen begins to perform oral on him.

Matt then stops working, and they have sex. After Moreen is satisfied, Matt resumes construction on the shelter. The first and most important part of the shelter is building a good cover. Matt creates a good cover, and after he gets the bamboo securely on the shelter, he lathers the top of it with palm tree ends.

After he is done building and as the sun is setting, he goes for a dip in the water for a few hours, and Moreen goes with him. As they are in the water, the arousal comes back. So, they attempt to have a little bit of intercourse, which was a bit hard. Then Moreen offers to experiment with something else, by saying, "I have never done the ass, but heard some friends tell me that they enjoyed it." Matt responds, "I have heard from women that like it and women who don't, the pain can be excruciating. Plus, that is something that would be hard to do in the water." "Well, let's get out of the water and do it," Moreen said, so, they exit the water and lay on the wet and lukewarm sand, and they tried it. With them lying on their sides, Matt pits it into her very tight butt hole. At first, Moreen feels pain; however, she does not want him to stop. After a little bit, Matt pulls out, and Moreen rolls on her back to allow Matt to nut on her boobs.

After they are done, they walk up near the shelter, and as the sun is mid-way on the horizon, Matt starts a fire for them to sit around and begin eating and drinking. Matt also tells Moreen, "It's been 39 hours; you can now try and make some clothing." Moreen responds, "I might make only a skirt tomorrow, but I don't mind being naked, and I'll be staying naked the rest of the night." It rained most of the night and in the morning. With it being so moist because of the rain, a lot more bugs come out. As they were asleep, they were being feasted on by insects. When they wake up the following morning before sunrise, they both start itching a lot as they have a lot of bug bites on them but cannot see them yet, due to how dark it still is. So,.they both hop up and go take a dip into the water to smoothen the itchiness.

They sit on the shoreline, waist-deep into the water, until after the sun fully rises. They then stand up in the water and look at themselves. Their upper inner parts of their legs have bug bites all over them. "O my God," says Moreen." "Yeah, what the hell. We need to make some sort of skirts for ourselves." Matt says So, they right away make them. Matt did not want one, and Moreen kind of did and did not, but due to the problem with bugs, they both felt like it was necessary. Matt and Moreen spend the first few hours of the mid-morning, on the beach in the hot sun making bottoms and a blanket.

After Matt and Moreen are done making them, they take a dip in the water before they put them on. Their time in the water lasts for a while. They swim for an hour then sit on the shoreline for another few. After they exit the water, they put them on, they eat a bit, and then go for a hike around the island.

During their hike, they went to parts the island they never saw before and came across a wooden cabin. The Cabin is in the semi-middle of the island, but it was a mile from any water. They stop there at the cabin and look at it before continuing to hike further. Hours later, as they were walking back to the shelter, they passed by the cabin again. "I like that cabin. It could provide us with a much better shelter then we have over out on the beach." Matt said as he kept thinking of ways to fix up that cabin and build a small lake. "Ok, I agree, but A: the roof of it is half gone, and B: it's more than half a mile away from the water. Where we spend a lot of time." Moreen says to Matt.

Back at the shelter, as the sun is setting, Matt and Moreen eat and talk for a little bit about the cabin. After some hours, they both lay down to get some sleep. It starts to rain overnight, and it wakes them up, keeping them awake for a couple hours of the early morning. As its raining, they try to lay there as comfortable as possible buy cuddling up, and they end up getting a few more hours of rest.

The next morning Matt wakes up before Moreen and goes back to where the cabin is and starts constructing the pond. He spends 5 hours straight on digging and has dug 1 foot deep at 9 square inches around. After the first five hours, he goes back by the shelter and rinses off in the water. Moreen asks, "Where you been?" Matt replies, "That cabin area, I'm setting it up for us." He said, then gets out of the water and goes to eat. Matt spends an hour and a half eating and resting and then goes back to dig for another 6 and a half hours.

By the end of the day, the pond is 3 square feet wide, 2 feet deep, and 6 square feet long. As the sun is setting, Matt gets back to the shelter and is very exhausted, so he goes right to sleep. Moreen is still wide awake as it is still very early. So, she hangs out in the water alone for a while, and when it gets later into the night, she goes to the shelter, has some food, and then goes to lie down. Matt awakes shortly after Moreen falls asleep, and it is about midnight.

As it is hot, Matt finds it hard to sleep and lays there with Moreen for an hour before getting up and walking out to the water. Under a dim night sky, Matt sits in the water on the shoreline alone. "My trip was fun up until we landed here. I wonder how long it will be before Moreen and I get rescued. I wonder if I'm gone

for too long will I have a job back home."
He thinks to himself. After about an hour, he
goes back to the shelter, lays down, and finally
dozes off to sleep.

A few short hours later, Matt wakes up
before the sun came up. Matt lays there for a
bit, hoping he will fall right back to sleep. But
after a while, when Matt does not, Matt finally
gets up and goes a few feet away from the
shelter and makes a fire so he could eat and
drank a little. Just as the sun comes up, he puts
out the fire and proceeds to walk to the cabin,
while Moreen is still asleep. He knows it will be
a hot day, so he does not bother putting on the
skirt he made for himself. Once he is at the
cabin, he resumes working on the pond. As it's
getting later into the morning, it got extremely
hot, and the heat is quickly getting to Matt.
However, he still pushes himself to work on the
pond.

Hours later, Moreen awakes and, not
wearing her skirt, wonders around the island
and finds Matt. "What are you doing?" she asks.
"As I said before, setting a better place for us to
stay, you'll see when it's all done." "Ok," says
Moreen, she then watches Matt for a moment
to figure out what he is doing, and then she

walks back to the shelter. With it still being mid-morning, she gets some breakfast. After having something to eat, she lays back down and tries to get another few hours of rest. After laying there for a bit, realizing she will not fall back asleep, she gets up and walks a bit and lays on the beach to tan before getting into the water and chilling there for a few hours.

After Matt spends these 6 hours, his pond is how he wants it; 15 square inches around and 4 feet deep into the ground. Now he must collect rocks to build a barrier around the perimeter. Before he does that, he goes back to the shelter and hangs out with Moreen. With Moreen already in the water, he joins her. About an hour later, they go up to the shelter. Where they eat and drink, and "play" a bit. Then as there are only a few hours of daylight left, Matt starts collecting rocks and gets 35% of the barrier built. Then he goes back to the shelter as the sun is disappearing off into the horizon and starts a fire. Matt and Moreen then go down to the water to hang out for hours. After getting really drunk, they exit the water and walk up the beach to the shelter under a bright moonlit sky. At the shelter, they both have one more drink and then lay down. With the light wind giving them chills, the lay in the

spooning position for body heat and dose off
into a deep sleep.

Matt sleeps in until mid-morning with
Moreen, but shortly after that wake-up, they
get a rain shower, which lasts for an hour. After
it clears up, Matt goes back to continue working
on the pond by the cabin. After a few hours, he
gets done building the barrier. He then creates
a stick floor and a wall on the inside, so water
does not turn to mud, so, to try to prevent that,
he built layers and tied them together then
layered the stick floor with leaves. After an hour
of layering, he dumps more water, and his plan
works. So, he leaves it like that and quits
working on it for the day.

Matt then goes back to the shelter as
the sun is setting and relaxes. When the sun
sets the moon well lights up the island, so Matt
and Moreen go for a night swim for about an
hour and then lay on the beach. As they lay on
the beach, Matt starts to caress Moreens'
breasts, and Moreen begins rubbing Matt's
dick. When Matt gets hard, she gets on her
knees and starts to perform oral. After a few
minutes, Matt lays down, and Moreen sits on
him with her boobs facing him and his dick
inside the butt. They then stay in that position

until they both cum. Afterward, they walk to the shelter and drank for a little bit before falling asleep in a spooning position.

The next day Matt works on filling water into the little pond he made. He first makes jugs to carry water in and then starts the process. To avoid running his skirt with water or having it ripped, he takes it off as he is going back and forth with water. Moreen gets up after Matt has been doing it for hours and asks, "Want help?" "If you want, yes." Moreen starts helping, and after the first few trips, she is hot, and her skirt is messing up. She then stops to take it off and then continue. As Matt and Moreen pass each other on trips, Matt thinks she looks cute running as she is naked, and her medium size breast are bouncing. It takes them approximately 6 hours to fill up their new pond, and after they are done, they both go back to their shelter and relax.

With a few hours left of daylight, Moreen goes in the water to swim, while Matt sits in the shelter and thinks about something. "He is surprised that he never but should of, considered a while ago, to go back to the plane and use its radio to get help. So, as Moreen is in the water, Matt goes back to the plane to use its radio to get help, So then Matt quickly exits the shelter and runs off. Matt walks back to where the plane landed, which was a 2-mile walk. When he gets to the sight, all he sees is a big grassy area and the first shelter he made. He walks over to where the plane was and looks up at the clear blue-sky thing to himself why, why, why, then he kneels, putting his head in his hands.

After a few moments sitting there, he notices arrows carved into a few trees. So, he then walks in the direction they point. After going half a mile, he sees more trees with arrow carvings and follows them for like 2 miles. He then finds himself standing in the middle of a field with trees surrounding it and a creek with a waterfall. He likes this new discovery and never expected to see this view on this island.

Meanwhile, miles back on the beach, Moreen is swimming, she then looks out in the distance and sees a boat. As the boat gets closer, she waves at it. However, even though it appeared to be closer, it was about 10 miles away. Moreen stares at the boat as it makes it turn away and disappears. After Moreen has been swimming for a few hours. she is tired, so they go sit on the shoreline for a while.

As the sun is setting, Matt arrives back from his journey and gets into the water with Moreen. "You were gone for hours," Moreen says as they are in the water with the sun setting in front of them. "I went to explore more and back to the plane to look for something. I couldn't find it, though." Matt says. After a bit more conversation, they walk out of the water, and Moreen has a seat on the sand. "I'm going to get drinks for us to have," Matt says, as he runs past Moreen and to the shelter.

As the sun is halfway down on the horizon, Matt returns, and they start drinking. The two of them sit there on the beach for a few hours and the island is well light up by the moon of the summer night sky. With the reflection of the moon on the water, Moreen and Mat choose to go further into the warm water. They swim for about an hour, as they are in the water, they spend a lot of time touching each other. Matt spends a lot of time caressing Moreens breasts and Moreen rubs Matts dick.

Then after hours of being in the water Matt and Moreen exit. After getting each other aroused, Matt follows behind Moreen with a hard-on, as they walk up onto the shelter,

Moreen keels down and with matt standing in front of her, she starts oral. Moreens does oral for a few minutes and then lays on her back on the wet sand. Matt then kneels and puts his hard dick into her pussy. They have sex for about 15 minutes, then when they are done, they walk back to the shoreline and drink more. As they have a couple more drinks, they enjoy the water splashing on them and gaze up at the bright night sky.

Close to midnight, they begin to walk back to the cabin, and out of nowhere, it starts to get windy. "I think a storm is coming," said Matt. "I know because it just got really windy out of nowhere," Moreen replies, they get back to the shelter and sit there enjoying the wind. They have a few more drinks and then go lay down. Soon after they lay down, the rain comes as they dose off to sleep.

After a couple hours of rest, they awake in the middle of the night. The rain is coming down very hard, and the sound of the pouring rain is making it very hard to fall back asleep. So, they ley there for a but, cuddle and have intercourse. After Cumming, they think they could fall asleep, but they do not. So, after not going back to sleep, they both grab a few drinks and sit up under the shelter enjoying the sights and sound of a thunderstorm and the heavy wind blowing on their bodies. By nearly 4 AM, they have been sitting there for a couple hours are both drunk again, and the rain has calmed down. But they decide to hang out more and enjoy the wind so they walk out from underneath the shelter and sit on the wet sand. By sunrise, they lay back down and fall asleep.

By noon the next day, Matt wakes up eats very quickly, and then he walks outside and around the cabin to assist the wind damage and what he needs to do to the structure of it. Some of its walls are half missing witch is ok, but 65% of the roof is gone. However, the cabin is built between two huge trees. Matt works on redoing the roof, by taking some blown off a piece of wood and reusing it. As he is working on the cabin again, Moreen wakes up. She eats and then walks out to the cabin and see that Matt is working on it. As she sees that he is doing necessary repairs to the cabin, she goes alone for a walk around the island.

Moreen walks around to where the plane landed when she arrived and saw that the plane was no longer there; she was puzzled. She then looks around the area while standing in one place and thinks to herself, "Is this really the landing site?" As she looks around, she sees their first shelter and then knows she is in the right area. She then recognizes the arrow carvings in the trees, so she does what matt did and followed them. She follows them to the middle of the island to a lovely green field and a creek with a waterfall. As she is hot and tired from all the walking, she goes in the creek and hangs out for a bit.

As it begins to drizzle a bit, she exits the water and starts to walk back to the shelter. The drizzle then turns into a light rain shower. As it begins to rain in the middle of the afternoon, Matt stops working and hangs out on the cabin porch drinking. After him hanging on the porch alone and drinking a bit, Moreen appears from the side of the house. "You weren't on the beach? Where were you?" Matt asks. "Just exploring the island," Moreen says, as she walks onto the porch soaked form the rain. When the rain stops they walk back to the shelter.

As the sun is setting, Matt and Moreen are sitting directly outside of their shelter with a fire going eating and drinking. After an hour of them both sitting there naked and drinking, they both start getting aroused. Moreen begins oral on Matt and his dick gets harder and harder. After like 5 minutes, Matt gives Moreen oral for a few minutes. Then Moreen lays on her back, and Matt puts his rock-hard cock inside her, and they have vaginal and anal intercourse. Moreen says, "Ram me as hard as you can. Fuck me so very hand, and I don't care how bad it hurts." So, Matt gives it to her as hard as he can. Moreen screams and moans very loudly and yells, "Don't stop, fuck me!" and it lasts for nearly an hour. After orgasm, Matt keeps his dick inside of her until it gets soft and falls out. They both feel fantastic and satisfied as they fall sound asleep right after they finish. They fall asleep in a spooning position with Matts arm around Moreen and his hand, cupping her boob.

Matt and Moreen both sleep a solid 7 hours without once waking up, for Matt, this is the first time he slept that long in a row. Matt felt good after getting that much solid rest. When they both woke up, they laid there for a few minutes. As they lay are awake, Matt says, "Can I rest my dick inside you for a moment." "Go ahead," Moreen replies. So, Matt put his dick in her ass but just lays there with it in her without thrusting. After a few minutes, he pulls out, and they get up and eat. The eat and hang out for about an hour before Matt headed to the cabin to work on it. Matt spends 5 hours working on the roof more and then it is done he walks to the shelter. Moreen is relaxing in the water as Matt arrives back on the beach. Matt decides to wait until the next day to start moving over because he is tired from working on the roof, and the sun is about to set.

Matt goes into the water with Moreen, and they play a little. As the sun is descending on the horizon, they get out of the water and walk up to the shelter and start a fire. They sit by the fire for a few hours, eating and getting drunk. After they are both really intoxicated, they go lay down in the shelter. They both very quickly dose off into a deep sleep. Matt gets up after a few short hours and feels very hot for some strange reason. So, with the bright moon lighting the beach, Matt grabs a drank and goes to the shoreline and sits in the water to cool off. After about a half-hour, he gets out of the water and goes back under the shelter. With Moreen still sound asleep, Matt has one more drank and then lays down. He falls asleep rather quickly and sleeps for a few hours.

Just before sunrise the next day, they both wake up. They eat fast and then start to move everything over near the cabin. Moving everything takes about an hour. Before there last trip taking belongs to their cabin, they went for a short dip in the ocean. After everything is moved, they test out the pond that Matt made. The pond was ok, but the water was denigrating little by little, so they spent an hour transporting water from the ocean.

Matt started before Moreen, so as one when to the ocean, the other was filling the pond. Each time they passed each other. Matt smirked as he was seeing Moreens boobs bouncing as she fast walks past him. After the pond is full of water they relaxed for a few hours in their newly built pond. In the pond, they spend a lot of time drinking and touching one another and touching is all they do for a while.

That night the moon shined very brightly, and it lit up the cabin, so Matt and Moreen got to sit inside their new cabin eating and getting drunk for a good while. After several hours both are drunk and lay down. When they lay down, they begin to cuddle, and that leads to more. After moments Moreen feels Matt's penis getting hard as is on her bare ass, "Just put it in," she says, "Pussy or ass?" asked Matt, "Put it in my ass, I like it." Moreen says. So, then Matt put it into her tight butt hole. They do that position for a few moments and then she gets on top of him sticking it in her butt. Moreen gets off him after she organisms and right before he does, so he nuts on her boob. They then touch each other for a second when they are done, they right away doze off.

Matt and Moreen wake the next day around noon. they eat something first to start their day and then walk around the island. They make it all the way to the other side of the island where they have never been before. However, it looks no different, and it was a 2-hour hike. Before they turn around and head back, they go for a dip in the water to relax and cool off. As they are in the water, they see a boat in the distance and stare at it.

They walk through the water approximately a mile of shore around the island, trying to follow the sight of the boat for miles, and then it moves far west. "Dammit, they didn't see us." Matt says, "yeah, fucken sucks." Moreen replies. hours later, still in the water, they walk the perimeter of the island back to their beach and sit on the shoreline. "Maybe we will see another boat in a few days." Moreen says, "I hope so," Matt replies.

As the sun is beginning to set, Matt and Moreen exit the water and walk back to their cabin, which given their current position, only takes them 45 minutes. As the sun is going down, tonight, there is a pleasant and cooling breeze, which feels incredible on their naked bodies. When they get to the cabin, they start a fire so they can relax outside. However, with the breeze, it is hard to start the fire, and takes Matt longer than usual, but he starts it and can keep it going. Matt and Moreen spend hours outside the cabin eating and drinking by the fire after hours of drinking, they have sex near the fire with the wind pleasuring them too.

As they are enjoying the night and the weather it starts to sprinkle, it does not bother them, and they still sit out by the fire. As it sprinkles more and more, the fire disintegrates, and the rain starts to pick up. Matt and Moreen then take their drinks on the porch of the cabin but do not go inside because they still want to enjoy the wind on their bodies. As it is pouring rain, they stand there on the porch enjoying their drinks and the breeze. Matt says, "The wind feels so good, right?" "Yes, very good; the wind pleasures me just as good as your cock." Moreen replies. After some time passes, they begin to feel tired and decide to get some rest. They lay in this wooden floor in the corner of the cabin and cuddle.

As Matt and Moreen sleep through the night. The wind gets worse and knocks over a few trees, and one was very close to their cabin. Due to how drunk they are, that the sound of trees falling outside around them does not wake them up. The rain takes a break for a few hours in the early morning and they are still asleep. However, when they wake up around daybreak, it is pouring rain just like it was when they passed out, and the wind is blowing hard. "Well, I don't think we're going to be doing much today." Matt says, "I know this fucken suck, fuck it we can just sit here, get drunk, and fuck all day." Moreen says Matt and Moreen are now unknowingly in the middle of a tropical storm.

As they are in the cabin, having intercourse, a tree comes down, smashing through the cabin just 95-feet away from them inside the cabin. It falls in on them as they are fucking and they stop, as they are both scared and do not know what to do or expect next, as they looked at one another with confused faces. They now sit there in the corner of their cabin, looking at each other, not saying anything just wishing the rain and heavy rain would end. However, they endure these conditions for another few hours.

That evening as the sun is setting through the cloudy sky, the storm is subsiding, and right after dusk, the rain comes to an end. As the moon is full and very bright tonight, Matt and Moreen are both thrilled and run out of the cabin to go chill out on the beach drinking and hanging out in the warm water. The moon gives them good light. At around midnight they leave the beach and head to the cabin. Once at the cabin they have a bit of food and then fall asleep and get good sleep through the night.

The following morning as they awake, the sun is out and shining bright. The temperature is kind of hot, so they right away go from laying down inside and get into their little pond. They spend hours in the pond and only get out to grab drinks and thus get very drunk throughout the entire day, Hours into drinking, they both get really turned on, and Moreen bends over on the side of the pond and says, "Let's go." Matt stands behind Moreen, as Moreen has her ass in the air. Matt then makes his dick hard and then puts it into Moreens ass.

They proceed to have anal sex for 10 minutes, and then they get out of the water. Matt then lays down on his back in the dirt and grass. Moreen climes on top of him, and they continue intercourse a for a bit longer, stopping when Matt cums inside of her. As they are both dirty from lying on the ground, they walk out to the ocean.

As the sun is setting, Matt and Moreen go up on the beach near their old shelter and make a fire. They sit around it and begin eating and drinking. However, they do not drink for much longer because they have been for nearly half the day and end up passing out sitting outside by the fire. As they are knocked out, sound asleep because of all the drinking, a rain shower comes through.

The rain pits out the fire but does not wake them. However, Matt and Moreen wake up in the middle of the night with no visible light, and it is tough to see, and the ground is very wet. "How are we going to get back to the cabin?" Moreen asks, "Let me get a bit more awake, and then we'll figure it out, just give me a few moments" Matt responds. Matt has a good sense of where the cabin is and the best path to take, so he holds Moreens hand to assist her as they carefully walk the half-mile and get inside the cabin. Once inside, they both sleep for the remainder of the night.

The next morning Matt wakes up early, almost right after sunrise. He spends time alone, he grabs a bite to eat before going outside, and in the pond, he made, enjoying himself while Moreen is still resting. Then Matt walks a few miles down the beach to explore a bit. Moreen awakes hours later and has a bite to eat before going alone on a hike through the island. After a few hours and walking deep into the middle of the island, she sits down on a fallen tree trunk for a while and spends time there enjoying the warm weather and nature. "This island is ok, but I hope I get rescued soon." She thinks to herself.

Meanwhile, Matt is miles back on the beach near the cabin. He walks into the cabin to look for Moreen. After a bit of not finding her, he grabs some drinks out of the cabin then walks back out to the beach where he drinks and basks in the hot sun for a few hours getting a tan. As he is tanning, he for some reason gets aroused and starts to masturbate.

As Moreen is sitting there in the middle of the island, she keeps thinking and thinking about her life. She thinks about how and when she will be able to get off this island. "I miss my old life, who knows when I will ever get off this island. I was so happy to start college, but now who knows if I'll be able to start in the fall like planned." She thinks to herself, as it is nearing 3 full weeks on this island. The thought of uncertainty is scary to Moreen. After spending time sitting alone thinking to herself for hours, she collects her mind. Then gets herself together and gets up to walk back. She sees a beach through some trees. So, instead of walking through the center of the island, which is a bit shorter. Moreen walks through the trees to the closest beach area and then swims in the water for 2 and a half miles to the main beach they stay close too. Then she walks to the cabin to get a snack.

At sunset, which is like an hour later Moreen walks to the beach, where she sits there alone for a bit. Matt sees her and walks over to accompany her. As Matt approaches her seated on the san, he has a boner. He stands by Moreen and she notices, so, she keels and puts Matts dick into her mouth. After a few moments, Matt kneels, and Moreen gets on all 4s, and Matt then puts his rock hard dick inside of her pussy. A couple minutes later Moreen says, "In my ass!" They both enjoy themselves having intercourse as the sun sets down on the horizon. They both finish after about a half-hour. They go back up to the cabin and drink for a while on the porch. After a few hours and having a lot to drink, they go into the cabin and lay down drifting off to sleep.

They both awake the next morning moments after sunrise but feel tired still. So, they ley there together for a while, touching each other until satisfaction is reached. Then in the middle of the morning, they both eat and then walk out to the water and get in. As they get to enjoy the water, the sky becomes very cloudy, and the warm sun begins to get hidden, and within less than an hour of enjoying the water, it starts to rain. In the hopes that it would pass over soon, Matt and Moreens continue to hang out in the ocean for a short time. However, after the rain not letting up for over an hour, they exit the water.

As they walk out of the water and onto the shore of the beach, the rain begins to come down more heavily. Matt and Moreen then walk back to the cabin and Moreen sits on the porch as Matt goes inside to grab them both a drink. They both sit there on the porch looking at the island landscape around them as they drink a lot, and the rain pours down on their island.

As Matt and Moreens sit on the porch drinking and watching the rain, Matt gets a boner. Moreen quickly notices and kneels on the hot wooden porch and puts Matt's man part into her mouth as he is sitting on a chair. After a few moments, she stands up and then sits down on his lap and puts Matt's penis inside of her. Moreen then rides Matt for a while as it is pouring down rain and very windy. Through the thunder and lightning of the storm, Matt enjoys the dim light exposing Moreens bouncing boobs as she is riding him. It lasts for a while, and when they finally cum in ecstasy, they then do more drinking. In the early evening, almost right after sundown, they are exhausted, drunk, and very sexually satisfied, so they go to lay down and dose off. However, with them falling asleep very early in the night, they get up only a few short hours later

At around 1 AM, Matt and Moreen both awake. They ley there for a bit to see if they would fall back asleep, but they do not. As it is hot in the shelter, they go outside, where there is a gentle breeze. Enjoying the breeze, they decide to go for a night swim in the ocean. Moreen goes down to the sea in front of Matt while he gatherers drinks to take out there with them. They swim in the water for a little over an hour and then sit on the shoreline and start drinking. They have an excellent relaxing time sitting there under a bright moonlit sky, feeling the wind and water on their bodies.

As it approaches early morning just before sunrise, they exit and make their way back to the cabin. With Matt and Moreen, both being drunk form all the drinking, they both walk with challenges and fall down a few times. They finally get back to the cabin as the sun is hitting the horizon. Once in the cabin, they immediately lay down. They then cuddle up together and fall asleep quickly. By the end of this new day, they have been trapped on this island for 3 weeks.

Meanwhile, off the island, Matt and Moreens friends and families have recently become concerned about them. Neither of them has any contact with anyone, and there has been no activity on social media, which is very odd for them both. The families have called the airline company, but it was no help. There was not even a record that the plane landed on the island. So now back on the mainland, there is a massive search effort going on while Matt and Moreen are stuck on the island that nobody has heard about

Ch. 5: weeks 4-7 on the island

Back on the island, Matt and Moreen are trying to make the best of it. Matt and Moreen have now been stuck on the island for 22 days, and most of the days are spent doing the same thing as previous days. Their 22nd day was a stormy day from the time they awoke. They woke up to a thunderstorm, that included very heavy rain, thunder, lightning, and heavy winds. So, they have no choice but to chill in the cabin, but at least they got to pig out on food and drink all they wanted.

The sun was out, but barely visible behind clouds, and the wind was up to 20MPH at times. During the storm, they sat in the doorway of the cabin for a while to enjoy the breeze. However, there were periods where the rain got to intense to want to sit by the door. As the sun was setting, the storm came to an end.

On their 22nd night, Matt and Moreen, even though they were both drunk, went outside. They then walk out and sit on a patch of sand near there cabin. They sit under a moonlit night sky and gaze at the moon and stars. As they sit on there, enjoying the pleasant breeze the storm system left, they see a shooting star, and Moreen, believing in wishes, makes one. She keeps her wish silent, and they both sit there for a little while longer. As it gets later into the night, they strolled inside the cabin, where they both fall asleep that night and get a good rest in.

The next morning Matt wakes up just as the sun is hitting the horizon, after eating a bit he goes for a hike around the island while Moreen is asleep. His walk through the island is peaceful, and he goes miles to another part of the island that he is never seen. While Matt walks through a small jungle of trees he sees water at the end. However, there is no beach and the ocean is not even with the land. In fact, he is standing on a cliff, and it is a 65-feet drop into the water. He thinks about jumping off the cliff and into the water, thinking it will be fun and exciting, but does not because he is tired from the hike and does not know how far of a swim it is to a beach.

So, as he is at the edge of the cliff, he sits on the warm and sticky grass and relaxes for a little bit doing nothing but thinking to himself. Matt thinks about what a life he is had thus far and how grateful he will be when he gets rescued from this island and back to his regular life. After resting to get energy, Matt begins a long hike back to the cabin. On the hike back, Matt takes a different route, walks along the edge of the cliff to the nearest beach, and then walking along the beach for a couple miles to the beach he recognizes.

When he arrives, it is the mid-afternoon and Moreen is awake walking around looking for him, Moreen sees Matt as he is walking up the beach and to the cabin. "Where the hell have you been?" Moreen asks, as she is concerned, and says, "I've been walking around the cabin and beach area looking for you for a while." "Sorry, I've been exploring the island, I woke up very early and wanted to do something different, it was a nice exploration," Matt says. Then Matt tells Moreen about the part of the island and suggests they go together sometime. "Can we go today?" Moreen asks. Matt, being exhausted, says, "I don't think so, it's quite a hike, but it might be a good place to watch the sunset sometime." Matt then lays down and doses off quickly while Moreen goes out to the water by their old shelter and chills there for a while.

Matt wakes up a few hours later as they have a few more hours of daylight and goes into the little pond to chill for a while. After moments he does not see Moreen and wonder where she is, but then 30 or so minutes later, she walks out from a distance and joins matt in the pond. As the sun is setting, like most nights, a fire is lit, and they have dinner sitting by the fire. They have a few drinks with dinner before going down to the beach.

Matt and Moreen take a walk to the beach and spends hours in the water. They swim for a bit and then sit on the shoreline drinking. The water is warm, and there is a light breeze in the air. After being tired of the water, they spend a bit sitting on the sand, enjoying the starlit night sky, and the pleasant wind, and do more drinking. As it gets late, they both become too tired to walk back to the cabin, so they decide to rest for the night in their old shelter on the beach.

As they awake the following morning, it is pouring down rain and a bit windy. They feel like going back to the cabin to eat, but they do not want to walk in the rain, so they decide to wait. Matt and Moreen sit there for an hour, and it is still raining hard; Matt says, "Let's give it a little more and see if it subsides." It does not, and after sitting there for nearly 2 hours, they decide to walk in this downpour back to the cabin.

When they arrive back at their cabin, they are both drenched, so Matt and Moreens on the porch until they are dry. They chose to dry off before going inside to reframe from getting the floor and the area where they sleep wet. It takes them a bit to dry, so as they sit there, they have some drinks that are stashed in a cooler on the porch. They end up sitting there for hours to enjoy the breeze, but the rain, however, has yet to let up, so after being on the porch for hours, they go inside. With it raining for hours on end through most of the day and evening, Matt and Moreen cannot do anything. So, they just stay in the cabin and rest. As they rest, they both dose off in the middle of the afternoon.

They wake up after a few hours have past and it is now the middle of the night. Matt walks out on the porch to see if it is still raining. It is, but its light rain and the moon in the sky is shining bright. Matt and Moreen both stayed awake and drank a little on the porch. As they sit there, they spend time talking about what each of them will do once they finally get off this island. Then after a few hours, right before dawn, they go back inside to try to get a little more rest. Matt cuddles Moreen and Moreen dozes off first, then after 5 minutes, Matt dozes off as well.

Matt and Moreen wake up mid-morning the following day and have something to eat, and then they go for a hike throughout the island. Matt shows Moreen the cliff and where he discovered it. The is approximately 3 miles northeast from the cabin, and the cliff is at the end of a small forest at the northeast corner of the island. At the cliff, they just sit there on the ledge with their legs and feet dangling off the ledge. After they sit there for a little while to take in the view and rest, they continue to hike through the island. Matt and Moreen continue walking on the ledge of the cliff for a mile until it ends and has a 25-feet drop onto a beach. So, they walk around the drop through the forest for about a mile and a half. Then walk out towards a beach. They then relax on the beach and in the water for many hours until sunset.

As the sun sets, they walk holding hands 2.5 miles on the beach back to their main section of the beach and then up

to the cabin, which is near the center of Back at
the cabin, Matt makes a fire for them to sit
around as they have dinner and drank for a little
while right outside the cabin. The weather is
warm and humid, and tonight they do not have
a gentle wind breeze. When they both are tired,
Matt puts out the fire, and they go into the
cabin and get some rest. Matt only sleeps for a
few hours and awakes just after midnight. The
island is darker than normal because the moon
is not shining that bright tonight, He feels wide
awake, so he goes for a walk to the nearest
beach, which is a mile where the old shelter is.
He goes into the water and relaxes in there for
almost an hour and then walks back to the
cabin to get more rest.

When Matt and Moreen both wake up
near mid-day, they find that they are in the
middle of another storm as it is raining heavily
and very windy. They sit on the cabin porch,
eating, drinking, and watching the storm. Matt
and Moreen sit on the porch for more than a
few hours, and each hour they hope it ends
soon. However, the storm lasts all day and into
the night. Matt and Moreen go to lay down as it
gets dark and dozes off. Late into the night,
they wake back up. The rain has stopped, and

the moon is shining very brightly on the island. Matt and Moreen decide to grab some drinks and go to the beach to hang out for a while.

Matt and Moreen first hang out on the sand for an hour and then go for a dip in the water. As they are in the water, they see another person swimming miles away but coming in their direction. As that person gets closer, Matt and Moreen hear someone say "Hi" to them as they are hanging in the water, near the shoreline. Soon the women arises from the water and looks about 25 years old. "Hi there, where are you coming from?" Moreen asks. She replies, "Florida, but swimming the ocean around the country." "Cool," Moreen replies. Moreen says "This guy and I have been stuck on this island for a while now, we were on a plane, but it landed her and then took off to early, so we missed it." The new girl and Moreen sit there shoulder-deep in the water for a few in the talking.

As they all get out of the water, the new girl notices that they are both completely naked. As they all sit on the beach, Matt excuses himself for a moment as he walks back to the cabin to grab some drinks. As it takes Matt about 15 minutes, Moreen and the new girl start talking.

As they talk for a few moments, the new girl asks with curiosity, "Aren't you going to put clothes on?" As Moreen continues sitting there for a while, she is still totally naked, and the new girl is sitting there with her looking at her breasts. "No, we have no clothes, and we are fine without them," Moreen replies. "What happened to your clothes?" The new girl asks, Moreen then explains about the genie and says, "We had to burn all our clothing to have unlimited food and drinks. Plus, most of the time, being naked feels good."

The new girl thinks the stuff about the genie is a load of shit. Matt returns to the beach with some food and drinks, and Moreen says, look as they have beers, liquor, sodas, and food in a cooler. "How do you think we got all this?" Moreen sarcastically asks. The new girl shrugs her shoulders without comment. The three of them then sit, drink, and feast.

After some hours sitting there eating and getting drunk, they all go back into the water around sunset, the new girl decides to take off her swimsuit as they walk to the water. When they exit the water, it is dark, but the moon is shining brightly, so it lights up the island very well. As they take their time walking back to the cabin, the new girl follows right behind them and is naked herself with her swimsuit in her hand. Matt then starts a fire, and they continue to drink for a while. Near the middle of the night, it begins to rain, and as it does, the fire goes out, and they go drink on the porch for like a half-hour before deciding to go inside and lay down. The new girl sleeps separately from the two.

The genie wakes them up right after dawn, saying, loudly, "I'm back!" Matt and Moreen wake up and are still very tired. "Ok, hears the deal," said the genie. "You have been in 2 tropical storms now, and there's a lot more to come. You will be stuck here for at least 36 more days. So, I have an offer, a well-built house with a creek in the center of the island, but Matt, you must donate 58% of what you currently have in the bank as well as feature income for one year. As for

Moreen 9% of what you will get once you get a job for one year. This will be automatically donated to the charity you tell me." Matt and Moreen both agree and decide on a charity and tell the genie. "O, and before I go, one thing, if that new girl stays on my island more than 22.5 hours from right now, she'll have to burn her swimsuit, or you'll both will lose everything." Says the genie before he disappears. Matt and Moreen lay back down and dose off for a few hours.

When they all wake up, hours later around noon the eat on the porch and chill, Matt asks the new girl if she is planning on leaving today, and she says maybe not. "Ok, burn your swimsuit." Matt says, "Why?" asks the new girl, Matt then tells her about the genie, and the girl says, "You guys are fucken crazy!" Matt yells "Get off my island now!" the girl replies "No!". As hours go by, the girl hangs out on the island with her swimsuit on, then Moreen gets as mad as Matt. "Leave our island now!" Again the girl replies "No!" Matt and Moreen give up asking and hang out for a few hours at the cabin. As it approaches sunset, they all venture out to the beach area.

As they do, Matt is behind the girl, and Moreen is distracting her by conversating. Once near the water, the girl removes her two-piece swimsuit right before making it to the water. Matt picks it up and runs away fast. Matt runs into the center of the island and makes a fire. It takes him a bit to start one. However, Matt gets a fire going, burns the girl's swimsuit, and puts out the fire.

Meanwhile, back on the beach, as both the girls look for Matt, he cannot be found and the girls do not want to be bothered with exhausting their energy. Also, Moreen knows what Matt is doing but plays along acting as if she doesn't. When Matt returns to the beach, Moreen asks, "Where did you go?" "I just had to check on some new project I'm doing in the woods," Matt responded while winking at Moreen. They all hang out in the water for a while. They swim for an hour and then when the sun begins to set they sit on the shoreline. When they get out, the new girl looks for her suit and when she cannot find it, she thinks its back by the shelter.

They all chill on the beach drinking, and after like an hour, they notice lights ways out. They then walk towards the light and end up on that green grassy land with the creek, that they have seen before. Matt and Moreen are then very excited and spend that night there. It is the house that the gene told them they would get. They were thrilled, and the house had lights at night because of the solar panels the house has on its roof and has a DirecTV Sattelite dish for TV enjoyment.

Matt, Moreen, and the girl spend the night there in the house and wake up in the morning right after sunrise. They all walk back to the cabin almost 2 and a half miles away, and when they arrive, the new girl looks for her swimsuit. When she does not find it, she starts asking questions, but Matt and Moreen ignore her. Matt and Moreen then go about their business away from the new girl and start moving their things down to the house. Their new home is not on the beach but has a creek right outside. It takes them 3 hours to get everything moved over to their new home. And as they are focused on moving everything, the new girl gets lost around the island on her own.

That night Matt and Moreen have a lovely time getting drunk. They spend half the night on a new beach area close to the house, and then half the night in their new house. As it gets late and they are drunk, they go lay down for a short time. In the middle of the night, Matt awakes and wants to go for a swim, he does, and it is pleasant outside. As it is warm, but not too humid and there is a gentle breeze.

Within an hour of Matt being on the beach, that new girl is spotted in the distance. It's the middle of the night, like 2 AM and she sees Matt in the water. At Matt gets out of the water and has a hard-on, the girl says, "Just give it to me." "What!" Matt replies. The girl says, " Sex! let's do it; however, you want." "Are you Shure?" asks Matt, "Totally," she says. Matt then has fun with her for a while on the beach. Then the girl walks back to the house and goes inside. Matt stays out on the beach for a bit, reflecting on what just occurred before going back to the house. With a lot on his mind after what just happened, he lays beside Moreen and goes back to sleep.

The next mooring mid-morning, everyone wakes up. The girl leaves Matt and Moreen without saying a word and wonders throughout the island. At the same time, Matt and Moreen spend time enjoying their new home setting stuff up, and enjoying a meal. As the new girl explores the island alone for a while, she discovers the cliff of the island; she loves it and takes in the lovely scenery before jumping off the cliff and into the water. She then swims away, not returning to the island. Back at the house, Matt and Moreen have a good morning meal and do a bit of mid-morning drinking.

After relaxing for hours cooped up inside the house, when midafternoon came, Matt and Moreen went out to the beach to chill in the water for a while. They chill out in the water for an hour, and by the second hour, they see a boat in the distance. They jump up and down, wave, make noise, and even swim out a bit, but like before, the people on the boat do not see them, and it veers off away. The swim is a mile to try to get noticed, but they do not, so they end up swimming back to their beach and sit in the water for a while.

Around sunset, as the warm sun is going down slowly on the horizon, they exit the water. Moreen sits on the beach as Matt walks over to the house to bring drinks out to the beach. They begin drinking, and after Matt takes a few sips, he starts a fire. They wanted to chill outside and over on the beach because it became windy, and the wind felt amazing on their bodies. They got to enjoy a good amount of the evening on the beach in the peaceful windy weather getting drunk.

After a couple of hours enjoying themselves sitting out on the beach, it started to drizzle. They both got mad because that was a sign that a storm was coming to ruin their night. Then within minutes of the drizzle, it started to rain. As it rained, they sat there for a few more minutes until it became too much and then went to the house and sat on the porch. They sat there drinking and chilling out for an hour until the storm got worse. They went inside, and with nothing more to do, they got drunk. After drinking for a good hour they sexually played for an hour or two before dozing off to sleep.

The next day, day-32, Matt and Moreen awake in the mid-morning, and it is pouring rain outside and very windy. After Matt and Moreen eat a little, they go out on the porch with some soda to drink and watch the rain and enjoy the feeling of the wind. They sit on the porch for a couple hours, in hopes that this system will pass. However, it does not, and it becomes windier and windier, and the rain gets heavier.

Once the wind becomes too much to bear, they go inside. Matt and Moreen then sit inside and talk and drank for hours. "I can't wait until the day we are rescued from this island." Moreen says, and Matt says, "Me either." "But what's going to happen when we do? We have no clothes, I'm cool with being naked, but we can't return to civilization naked." Moreen says. "I don't know, hopefully when we do get rescued, there is spare clothing available. I have clothing that could be sent to me once back on land and somewhere safe." Matt replies, Moreen says "I also have extra clothes somewhere." "What were you going to South Florida for?" Moreen asks, Matt replied. "I was going for my last month of vacation. South Florida is one of my favorite vacation destinations."

As hours go on and the rain does not subside, they both try to think of being more creative to pass the time, however, they are both far from creative individuals and fail to come up with ideas. They then both sit there for hours more and hang out and drank. Out of boredom, Moreen decides to ask Matt if they can just go lay together and fool around. "Yeah, nothing else to do," Matt says, then they walk to their sleeping area.

In the middle of the afternoon, they both take a nap but wake up after a few short hours and woke up around sunset. When they awoke, the rain had stopped, but the wind was still blowing strong. Matt and Moreen took a walk outside for a little while, but walking was challenging with the wind blowing against them. However, during their short walk, they saw a few trees knocked down, but thankfully they were far enough away from their house.

As Matt and Moreen go back inside to chill out, they come to realize the girl that was on a swimming journey has not been around for a while. They knew she went for a walk to explore the island however, that was nearly 2 days ago. So, with 2 days of not seeing her, Moreen wondered what may have happened to her. Moreen asks, "Have you seen that one girl? I just realize I haven't." Matt replies, "I haven't either; I think she probably got tired of this island and continued her swimming journey." "You could be right about that." Says Moreen. Then they just talk about random things as they then chill out in the house for a few hours more before laying down and getting some sleep.

The next morning, right after dawn, Matt and Moreen awake. They spend a bit of time having breakfast and relaxing in the house before going to hang out on the beach. They spend about 20 minutes sitting on the warm sand, then Matt and Moreen go into the water. Close to noon, after hours in the water, it starts to get windy, and then a few minutes later, it began to drizzle. They sit in the water for a few more minutes and then knowing that a storm was approaching, Matt and Moreen walk out of the water and go chill out in the house and on the porch.

When Matt and Moreen get in the house, they dry off and then prepare and eat lunch. Afterward, when they are finished eating, they get a few drinks and head back outside. As they sit there on the porch, they talk for a little while getting to know each other more.

Matt asks Moreen to tell him something about her that he does not know. "I just turned 18 days after our flight left Vegas," Moreen says, Matt then replies, "O shit! I'm 28 and thought you were older, I'm sorry." "It's ok, everything that has happened here will stay here. I hope we get off this island soon because I'm supposed to start college at the end of summer." Moreen says, and Matt replies, "My vacation from work is supposed to be over by now. I work as an investor in New York City. Where are you going to school, and for what?" "A school in South Florida and I think I want to get into education." Moreen says, and Matt replies, "That's cool and it a rewarding career. What made you choose that profession?" "I like education and think it's highly important," Moreen replies. "I have my degrees in business and finance," Matt says. They then sit on the porch a little bit longer and drink, as the sun is setting behind all the clouds the storm begins to subside.

As the sun is setting, Matt and Moreen walk out to the beach with some drinks and sit on the wet, cold sand, and matt starts a fire. After 25 minutes, they go into the water and swim for almost an hour. Once they get tired of swimming, Moreen sits on the shoreline while Matt goes up to the house, fills a cooler with soda, liquor, and beer, and then drags the cooler of drinks a quarter-mile to the beach and down to the shore and sit there under a bright moonlit sky drinking as they enjoy the wind and waves splashing them. After a few hours after they are intoxicated, they walk back to the house and right away go inside to lay down for the night. They doze off not long after lying down.

Matt awakes as the sun is coming up, and Moreen is still very sound asleep. As Matt sits outside of the house thinking to himself, he thinks about building a hammock and extending the porch. He thinks he is got a pretty good idea on how to build a hammock and an extension to the house. The extension he is thinking about building will have the porch extended out by 6.5 feet long and 5 feet wide. The expansion will be on the left side of the house. Matt then walks back to their old cabin and start dismantling some things, as he does, he sees that his man-made pond is nonexistent. The dismantling of the old cabin takes Matt a few hours, and after he is done, he starts dragging pieces of it about a mile to the middle of the island where the house is. When he first approaches with the first batch, Moreen is up and standing on the porch and says, "What are you up to now?" "A new project," Matt replies.

He then lays down a batch of wood and goes back to the cabin to grab another batch. After his second trip between the new house and the old cabin, Matt takes a couple hours to relax. He first goes into the house and gets some lunch before going to the water and hanging out with Moreen. They hang out for a little while, and then Matt exits the water to go do some construction work. Within 5 hours, Matt builds onto the porch extending the porch 4 feet in length, and 2 feet wide witch is close to half of the goal. Matt quits working on the project for today and spends what is left of the afternoon and evening with Moreen.

Matt wants to fulfill the promise he made days ago to Moreen and take her up to the cliff to watch the sunset. As the sun begins setting, like not being directly over them, they go in the house to eat for a moment. Matt then gets the cooler and fills it up with drinks and says to Moreen, "let's go for a hike." Moreen replies, "Ok." Then Matt and Moreen hike quickly through the island and to the cliff. They sit on the ledge and they spend close to 2 hours sitting there, drinking, and watching the sun disappear into the horizon.

Matt and Moreen look at each other under a bright moonlit sky, then jump off the cliff and into the water. They then swim around the perimeter of the island and it takes them over an hour to swim back to the part of the beach close to their house. When they approach the shore and walk out of the water, Moreen sits there, on the sand and Matt goes to grab a few drinks for them to enjoy. Matt and Moreen then sit there on the beach for a bit before feeling tired and walk back to the house to get some rest. They lay down right after arriving at the house. As they lay there, they cuddle, and Matt raps his arm around Moreen cupping her boob and within moments they both doze off and sleep soundly through the night.

The following morning, Matt and Moreen both wake up right after the sunrise. Matt's hand is still on her boob as they awake. They both lay there for a few moments until they feel fully awake and continue to snuggle. Then they walk to the kitchen to have breakfast. After they eat and hang out together for about an hour, Matt says, "I have to go back up to the cliff to get our cooler and then work on my project." As he walks away. Matt first runs to the cliff, gets the cooler, and runs back with it. Back at home, he rests for 25 minutes and then to continue his project, just outside the house. It takes Matt a few hours to think of a good spot to build the hammock. After he finds the ideal spot, he right away begins to build. Matt then completes the making of the hammock within a couple hours. Moreen enjoys it for a few hours as Matt works on part two of the project, extending the porch.

Matt plans on finishing his project by days end, but within moments of starting to work on the construction of the porch, it becomes very windy and starts to rain. So, with Matt barely getting anything done, he stops. Moreen then walks up from the beach to the porch, where she and Matt chill for a few hours drinking. As the sun sets, the rain shower turns into a powerful storm, and with the weather getting more intense, Matt and Moreen go inside the house for the night.

In the house, they pig out on food and get drunk for a few hours. After a while of Matt and Moreen drinking heavily, they feel tired and go lie down to get some rest. In the middle of the night, Matt awakes, feeling an abundance of energy. Matt then walks out to the porch to see if it is still raining because there is no more storm like noises anymore. As he walks to check, he grabs a drink. He then stands there on the porch for a bit and sees that it is not raining, and the moon is shining brightly, so he then walks out to the beach and goes for a dip in the water.

After a half-hour, Moreen awakes and does not see Matt next to her. So, Moreen walks through the house and when she does not see him inside around the house. She walks outside, and with the moon shining brightly, she has a sense that he is out chilling in the water at the beach. So Moreen grabs the cooler and drinks and lunges it out to the shoreline. She then joins Matt, and they swim for a while, then sit in the water on the shoreline and do more drinking. As the sun rises in the skyline behind them, they walk back to the house, go inside, and get into bed, they then cuddle up together, and they both doze off to sleep.

A few short hours later Matt and Moreen both awake together around noon. As they wake up, they fell tired and lay there for a bit more; when the too finally get up out of bed, they walk to their kitchen to prepare lunch and spent time eating together for a bit. Matt then says, "I have to go, so I can finish my new project." Then he goes right away off to resume work on his project, which is right outside. He spends 3 hours working on the porch expansion. As Matt works on the last phase of the project, the porch, Moreen, hangs out in the creek. After a few hours of working, Matt needs a rest and goes to join Moreen in the creek.

After Matt and Moreen hang out in the creek for a couple hours, Moreen exits the water, she goes into the house to grab them each a drink and after one drink she goes to lounge in the hammock. Moreen really enjoys it and dozes off in it. As she rests, Matt works a bit longer on improving the porch of the house, and after a few hours, as the sun begins to set, his project is completed.

Matt walks out to the beach and then sits on the shoreline to watch the sunset. As Matt is sitting on the shoreline, Moreen wakes up from her nap, with no sign of Matt she gets out of the hammock and walks to the beach and joins him. After the sun is down, the night sky is not as lit as the previous night's, so Matt goes on the beach to start a fire. It takes a while, because of the wind to start. However, once it is lit, they try to enjoy the beach. However, after 30 minutes, it begins to rain. They think it will mess up their night, but as it rains, Matt and Moreen continue to sit on the beach in hopes that the rain passes quickly, and it does.

After it stops raining, Matt and Moreen go sit in the shoreline of the water and drink for a while. "The wind after the storms always feels incredible on our naked bodies, am I right?" says Moreen, "Yes!" Matt replies. They then spend the next few hours sitting there and drinking. Moreen says, "I see you're a bit excited; do you want to?" "Of course," Matt replies, and then they have fun, it lasts a half-hour, and then they walk back up to the house. At home, they stand on the porch together, having a midnight snack, and then go into the house and dozes off.

Matt only rests for a few hours and wakes up in the middle of the night. When he does, he drinks a bit more and goes for a dip in the creek. The weather outside is warm, even at around 3 o'clock in the morning, but there is a light breeze. Matt stays in the creek for a bit over an hour, then goes back inside the house and goes to sleep.

The following morning Matt and Moreen wake up about the same time, in the mid morning. They eat a quick meal and then go on a hike together around the island. After a few hours, they have gone about 3 miles, and they were standing at the exact location where the plane landed the first day they got there.

Matt and Moreen then sit down on the hot sticky grass to get some rest. As they sit there, they both reflect on their life before they got on the island. "My job gave me a 2-month vacation, which is the longest vacation I've ever had. Before we landed here, I was about 3 and a half weeks into my vacation." Matt said, then Moreen replied, "Cool, I just graduated high school 3 weeks before we got here, and on my way to move into a university down near Miami." After an hour or so, sitting there, they begin to walk back to the beach where their house is.

The walk back took them a little less time because they took a different route. When Matt and Moreen arrived back at home, they had a bite to eat and a drink before going into the water to cool off for a while. They hung out in the creek for an hour, and then Matt goes up to the house, after they are done swimming they get out and he gets a cooler full of drinks. Then they walked over to the beach and sat on the shoreline for a few hours until after sunset.

After sunset as matt is slightly drunk, he feels tired and goes to lie down on the sand. Moreen is not drunk because she is only drinking soda, she stays in the water and swims a bit more. However, shortly after she starts swimming, it begins to rain. Meanwhile, Matt does not fall asleep but just lays there and rests for about an hour. With the rain picking up, Matt and Moreen quickly leave the beach and go back to the house. Once at the house they sit on the porch enjoying the sights and sound of this nighttime thunderstorm.

As they sit, the wind picks up after an hour, and it feels good. After sitting there for a few, Matt starts drinking more, and Moreen has a few drinks. After a few hours pass, they finally go inside the house and fall asleep.

The next morning Matt awakes in the early. However, he continues to lay there in the hopes that he will fall back to sleep. After a bit, when he does not, he gets up and goes to the kitchen and gets something to eat to start his day. Meanwhile, Moreen is still sound asleep. Then he grabs some soda and walks out on the porch. It is daylight but still raining and very windy. He sits there drinking some soda and watching the rain as it comes down hard and enjoys the breeze of the wind, which feels fantastic. An hour after he is sitting there, Moreen wakes up and walks out to the porch.

She says, "Good morning," and sit there with him for a few minutes. After a few moments sitting there, Moreen walks inside and making herself breakfast. After she eats, she goes back out on the porch and sits with Matt waiting for the rain to stop. As they sit there, they talk to one another, more disclosing, more about each other to each other. Moreen then tells Matt, "I was in foster care from age 9 until we left on the plane." "I'm sorry to hear about that. I know about foster care because when I was in my teenage years, my parents did foster care. Matt then had a flashback (Matt's parents decided to do foster care.

They discussed it with Matt, first and matt did not mind but he was confused about it at first as to it changing his home life. Matt and his family lived in a lovely 6-bedroom house, so his family took in 3 or 4 kids at a time. Matt's mother stopped working her job in a nursing home and stayed home.)

As they talk more Matt says "I was always the oldest form the kids we got and had to set a good example. Did you have good homes?" Moreen replies, "Most times, yes, but my last few months in the system, I was in a group home because the family I was with quit foster care and moved out of state. I had the option to be adopted and go, but I refused." Moreen replied.

After some passing hours, the rain stopped, and the bright sun came out to shine. However, the rain system left behind some strong winds and waves in the water. Matt and Moreen both take a short walk to the end of the beach and get a bit wet in the water. However, because of the waves being intense, they just get into the water up to their knees. They also

Do not stay in the water for more than a few minutes. After getting a little wet, they walk up the beach a few feet, and then Moreen sits down on the cool, damp sand while Matt walks to the house to go get a cooler of drinks.

Matt and Moreen then sit out there for hours, nearly the rest of the day on the beach drinking soda and more. Although the sun is shining brightly down on them, it is not that hot, with it being very windy. As the sun begins to set, it becomes very cloudy again. However, they continue to sit there for a few hoping the clouds will pass, and they can catch a lovely sunset. However, what they were hoping for does not happen, and it begins to rain. They get up from the sand after it is already raining hard and run to the house. Matt and Moreen sit on the porch for a couple hours, and after seeing that the rain will not be stopping any time soon, they go lay down.

Quickly after laying down, they both doze off. However, Matt wakes up just a couple short hours later. He then gets some beer and goes to sit out on the porch. It is still raining but not as hard as when they fell asleep. Matt sits on the porch for a couple of hours in the middle of the night drinking and, enjoying the feeling of the wind. Just before dawn, he goes back inside. Once he goes inside, he makes himself something to eat and then goes back to bed. He lays there awake next to Moreen for a bit before dozing off to sleep.

The next day Matt and Moreen both wake up around noon. They then leisurely stroll into the kitchen together and grab something to eat. They sit there, inside eating for about an hour Then go outside and hang out on the porch for a while, and Matt begins day drinking. Moreen then gets bored of sitting on the porch and goes into the creek. As she is in the water, she feels the smoothness of the warm water and light wind.

She likes this creek as its surrounded by trees and gives the feeling of seclusion. The water is warm like the weather, and it soothes her body. After a bit of Moreen chilling alone in the water, Matt joins her. As Matt walks off of the porch and into the creek, she watches him because she enjoys looking at his body. After Matt makes his way into the water, they both swim around the entire creek for an hour.

     With a few hours of daylight left, they choose to go out to the beach and watch the sunset. So, before they leave the house, Matt grabs a few drinks and brings them with them. They then walk a mile-half to the beach, and when they get to the ocean, they are sweety. So, they right away go for a swim for about an hour and then sit down on the shoreline. With the wind giving them a light breeze and the warm water splashing them, they chill out and watch the bright sun sail off into the horizon. They continue to sit there for a short time after the sun sets, and then they begin to walk back to the house.

     As they walk back to the house under a dim night sky, it starts raining. So, they begin to walk faster, and as they are sprinting through ab wooded area, Matt falls over a fallen tree trunk and really injures himself. Matt then lays here on the ground holding his right leg where the pain is. "Are you ok? Are you ok?" Moreen asks as she kneels beside him as the rain is pouring down. "I don't know I'm in a lot of pain," Matt says, He then gets up and with him in a lot of pain limps his way back home. Moreen walks beside him slowly in case he falls again.

After an hour of walking, they arrive back to the house, and Matt's leg is covered in dirt and bleeding. Moreen then helps him into a bathtub and, with no running water, fills the tub up with water by running out to the creek filling a bucket of water. It takes her 12 trips and an hour to fill the tub up with water, and then she helps Matt wash the dirt off his legs. Matt then gets out of the tub with Moreens assistance and lays in bed. As Matt lays in bed, he asks for Moreen to get him a few drinks, and she does. They then both sit there in bed for a while drinking. "How does your leg feel?" Moreen asks, "It still hurts bad," Matt replies. After they both had a few more drinks, they dozed off.

At about 1 AM, Moreen wakes up and feels wide awake. So, with Matt still asleep, she goes to the creek and hangs out in the water for about an hour. As she is in the water, the moon is brightly reflecting off the water, and it is very windy. By 3 AM, Moreen goes to lay back down, dozes off. She stays asleep for the rest of the night.

The following morning both awake mid-morning, and Matt is still in a lot of pain. Moreen then makes Matt some food and brings it to him in bed. "How are you feeling?" Moreen asks, "Like shit, I can't even move right now." Matt responds. They then both hang out in bed for a while and then with Moreen being bored, she asks, "Do you mind if I go for a hike for a bit?" "No, just bring me some drinks to last me for a while," Matt replies.

Matt spends all day in bed, and Moreen brings him a cooler full of ice and drinks to satisfy him. And then Moreen goes for a walk through the island. While laid up in bed, Matt drinks a lot and sleeps a lot. The pain Matt is in is barely bearable, so he tries to be asleep as much as possible. The house only has cooling fans, so he is not that comfortable which makes relaxing a struggle for him.

Meanwhile, it's around noon, Moreen goes for a dip in the creek for a bit before she starts her little adventure. She hikes around, in the complete nude, like usual for a couple of hours. She ends up at the cliff after hiking around. She then bathes in the sun as she lays on the cliff touching herself and enjoys a nice tan. After resting on the cliff for about a half an hour, she takes in the scenery, right before she jumps off and dives into the ocean down below. She then swims for about a mile and then makes her way on to a beach. However, the beach is still a couple miles away from the house. With there still being a few hours of daylight left, she sits on the beach, tanning again for a bit and watching the sunset off into the horizon. As Moreen hangs out there alone, she pleasures herself on the shoreline. And then as the sun is setting, she walks back to the house.

Once at the house, Moreen checks on Matt, and he is sound asleep. She then makes herself something to eat and after eating she goes to hang out and drink on the porch. After being on the porch for a bit, it begins to get windy. The wind feels good, but then a short time later, the wind picks up, and it begins to down poor. Moreen sits out on the porch for a bit longer until the wind becomes too intense, and then she goes inside the house. She then sits alone somewhere around the house for about an hour and thinks about her life. At around midnight she lays down next to Matt and falls asleep.

In the mid-morning, both Matt and Moreen awake. They lay there together for a bit and talk. With Matts leg feeling better, he gets up out of bed after 36 hours and attempts to walk to the bathroom. He limps a bit and is still in pain. So, he knows he will not be doing much besides lounging around the house, to rest his leg for another day. Matt hung out on the porch almost the entire day, Moreen hung there with Matt for a few hours and then went for a hike around the island.

By the mid-afternoon, Moreen hiked up to the beach on the other side of the island, where they've never been. After lying on that beach for a while, she swims a while around the perimeter of the island. Moreen stopped swimming after going a distance of 2 and a

137

half miles. At sunset, she sat on the shoreline but was a mile from their main beach. As the sun began to set, there came a light breeze that smoothened the air around her.

Meanwhile, back near the house, Matt got bored of being on the porch, so he carefully walked to get into the creek. The walk took him longer than usual due to the pain, but he was determined to get into the water. The warm water felt great as he sat there in the shallow part of it, and the light breeze felt soothing. Just after sunset, Moreen swims for a bit more going in the direction of their main beach. she reaches the beach close to home kinda quickly, where she sits and rests.

Meanwhile, back at home, Matt gets out of the creek after sitting in the water for a few hours. He relaxes for the rest of the night on the porch, drinking. As matt was sitting out on the porch, Moreen finally returned home at the end of the night, and they hung out on the porch for a few hours more. As it got later into the night, Matt was drunk, and then Matt and Moreen went into the house and went to sleep.

The next morning on about day 54, they both wake up a couple hours after sunrise. "My leg feels a hell of a lot better," Matt says as he walks around the house. Moreen replies, "I'm glad to hear, do you want to try and walk out to the beach later this afternoon?" "Yes," Matt says as they sit there in the house. As it approaches the late morning hours, they hang out on the porch drinking soda. When they get on the porch, they notice how cloudy the sky is. The light from the sun is a bit distorted as it sits behind many clouds, and it also is very breezy outside with there being strong wind gusts at times.

After a couple of hours of sitting on the porch, the wind does not calm down, and it gets cloudier. So, instead of them trying to walk out to the beach, they just chill in the creek. Matt and Moreen right away go get into the creek, while they still have time. The wind in the air and the warmness of the water felt sensational. They lounged in the creek for an hour and a half and then the rain started. As it starts to drizzle, they stay in the water for a few more minutes and, as they sit in the shallow water they have

133

another drink. They then exit the water and walk up the porch of the house.

As soon as they get underneath the porch, it begins to poor, and Matt sits down in a chair on the porch and watches the rain poor. Moreen goes inside the house for a few moments to get drinks and brings them out to the porch. They then sit there for a few hours drinking on the porch to watch and hear the sound of the rain and enjoy the heavy wind on their bodies. As the sun begins to set behind the clouds, the storm calms down and within a few minutes' stops. With it getting into the night, there's not a cloud in the night sky and the island is well-lit by the moon, they decide to go hang out on the beach.

With them feeling buzzed, they sit on the porch for a few moments drinking water, and then they grab some drinks and make their way to the beach, Although the moon is providing good light, they take their time walking slowly because Matt has just recovered for his injury. So, walking that half-mile takes them about an hour. Once at the beach, the two go swimming for a while and enjoy the semi-warm water. However, because of the storm that they just had, some of the waves are huge. So, they only swim 300 feet off the shoreline.

After swimming for close to an hour, they get tired and go chill out sitting on the shoreline. Matt and Moreen then sit there enjoying the night with some cold drinks, waves splashing their lower bodies, and the wind soothing them. After a few drinks and sitting there for a few hours, they decide to walk back to the house. They walk slowly like they did on their way there. By the time they get back to the house, it is the middle of the night, Moreen is tired, but Matt is not.

Matt then sits there alone on the porch while Moreen goes off to bed. Out on the porch, he enjoys a few more drinks and the elements of nature. After a few hours as it got into the early morning, Matt retreats to bed and is feeling good, relaxed, and drunk. As he makes his position into bed, Moreen awakes. They then cuddle up and fall asleep.

About mid-morning the next day, they both wake up, with Matt still tired from staying up late into the early morning, he stayed in bed and rested For a little while more. Moreen got out of bed and made herself something to eat. After cooking breakfast, she brings some to Matt. Then Moreen sat around the house, mostly in the front room. After about an hour enjoying her food and a soda, she is going for a dip in the creek.

As Moreen is relaxing in the water, Matt gets out of bed 20 minutes after she exits the house. Matt then goes to chill out on the porch. After an hour, he walks over to the creek where Moreen has been for hours. Matt then joins her in the creek, and Moreen right away asks, "How is the leg? How did you sleep?" "Well, the pain is gone, thankfully. Also, I slept well; I went to bed hours after you. Thanks for asking. What about you? How are you feeling? By the way, thanks for always taking good care of me, even though I am way older than you" Matt replies, Moreen says, "I am feeling ok, and you are very welcome. I just hope we get rescued soon from this island." "I hope so too," says Matt.

As they stand in the creek, they look up at the sky; it is clear and blue, with only a few clouds. The sun is brightly shining, and it's very hot with no breeze. So, the two stay in the water for most of the early to mid-afternoon. In the mid-afternoon, the sky becomes cloudy like it is about to storm, and Matt and Moreen get disappointed.

In the early evening, they go up into the house to have something to eat. After they relax and eat inside for an hour, they take some drinks and go out to the beach and watch the sunset. Like yesterday they take the time, and the walk takes about an hour. With the sun slowly setting, it's still very hot as they walk out to the beach. They become covered in sweat as the air is very moist and there is no breeze. They get to the beach just as the sun begins touching the horizon. So, with only an hour or so of daylight, they right away jump into the ocean to cool off. They watch half of the sunset standing in the water chest-deep. After feeling tired of swimming and standing, they sit on the shoreline with their lower bodies submerged in the warm ocean water.

As Matt and Moreen are relaxing, they open some drinks and watch the summer sun descend on the horizon. The temperature outside pleasantly drops as the sun sets, but it is still humid. As they sit there for a few hours, they look up at the sky and gaze at it. There is no full moon and the moonlight tonight is dim, the stars are bright, and they see a few passing planes flying high in the sky. Once again, like before, they see a shooting star, and Moreen makes another silent wish.

Moreen believes in this shooting star fairytale because when she was 8 years old, before being in foster care, her mom taught her that it was real. It became real when she wished one night that her dad became freed from cancer. Her dad was but died in a work-related incident. After the passing of her dad, her mom lost herself. She, in turn, became a huge alcoholic and started using meth, and that, in turn, made her no longer be able to care for Moreen. So, Moreen then went into foster care.

As it got late into the night and when they had no drinks left, they slowly made their way back to the house. By the time they got to their house, it was just after midnight. Matt and Moreen were not that tired, so instead of going in and going to bed, they went in to get more drinks and sat out on the porch for a while. Out of nowhere, it became very windy which felt great, but the wind made them believe a storm was coming, and they were right. A few minutes after the wind started heavy rain came pouring down. They sat there to watch, hear, and feel the wind and rain, but after about 30 minutes, it became unbearable, and they went inside the house. With it being late and them having nothing to do, they laid in bed, drinking a few more drinks before calling it a night and going to sleep.

Shortly after sunrise the next morning, both Mat and Moreen awake. Feeling well-rested, they get up and make themselves breakfast. After making breakfast, they stand there in the kitchen, eating and talking. "How are you feeling?" Moreen asks, "Good," Matt responds. After a few hours of staying inside the house, they walk out on the porch. It is scorching and humid, they do not stay out there long. By the mid-afternoon, after drinking for a bit, they run off the porch and dive into the creek. They both swim in the creek for a few hours, the water feels soothing to them as it is burning up outside. After hours of swimming, the sky above becomes cloudy.

In the mid-afternoon under a cloudy sky Matt and Moreen exit the creek and go chill on the porch of the house. After making it on to the porch, Moreen sits down while Matt goes inside the house and grabs some drinks. After a few moments of them sitting on the porch, it starts to rain just like they predicted.

As the rain was pouring down, Matt and Moreen continued to sit on the porch, watching it rain. The rain shower lasted a couple hours, and just before sundown, the rain stopped, and the sky became clear. The rain made it feel hotter, but Matt and Moreen decided to hike through the island with a plan to watch the last bit of sunset on the cliff. With the sun slowly setting, they hike about 3 miles through the center of the island. Feeling tired and with very hot and humid, they sit on the ground to rest for 30 minutes before hiking the half-mile up to the. After 25 minutes they reach the cliff just as the sun touches the water in the distance. They watch it set as they sit on the edge of the cliff, with their bare butts sitting on sticky grass and their legs dangling over the cliff.

About an hour after the sunset, they jumped off the cliff and into the warm ocean water. With the moon lighting up the summer sky, they swim around the island until they reach their home beach. When they reach it, they sit on the shoreline to rest for close to an hour. After resting, they walk back to their house,. As soon as they get into the house, they get a drink. After they have a drink inside, they load drinks into a cooler and go out on the porch and enjoy them. They then sit there on the porch for hours getting drunk together.

As it approached midnight, they both were drunk, and they stumbled into the house. Moreen right away fell asleep while Matt chose to hang out and drink more around the house. After getting more drunk in the house, Matt and Moreen go lay in bed and fall asleep almost instantly. Matt, however, only sleeps for a couple hours and wakes back up.

As it is around 3 in the morning, Matt is wide awake and cannot fall back asleep. Matt then decides to go outside and take a dip in the creek. He enjoys being in the warm water under a dim summer night sky as he swims for about an hour. Just before daybreak, he goes back inside, and as Moreen is still sound asleep, he lays back down. Matt lays there, still feeling wide awake for a few more moments. Then after getting in a comfortable position, he finally dozes off.

Just before noon on their 42nd day on the island, Moreen and Matt wake up. They spend a few moments in bed relaxing before getting up and starting their day. When they finally end up getting out of bed, they slowly stroll into the kitchen and make themselves something to eat. They spend about an hour in the kitchen eating before making their way outside and onto the porch.

Close to noontime, Matt and Moreen are sitting there on the porch. They are enjoying the sights and sounds of nature around them. The sun is brightly shining as there are only a few clouds in the sky, and there is a soothing breeze of wind that is consistently blowing. After a while chilling on the porch, Matt goes alone to dive into the creek while Moreen, still feeling tired, strolls back into the house and lays back down in bed.

Moreen quickly doses back off to sleep while Matt chills for a bit longer in the creek. Being in the water feels sensational as it is nice and warm, and the breeze of the wind blows above it. Hours later, Matt exits the water and goes back into the house. He searches the house and finds Moreen sound asleep. So, Matt lets her sleep and goes back outside and sits on the porch for several hours, drinking.

Just before sunset, Matt chooses to walk down to the beach to watch the sunset. Shortly after he leaves the house, Moreen gets up. Moreen looks for Matt around the house and then outside. With no sign of him, she assumes that he is at the beach because the sun is setting. So, Moreen quickly makes herself something to eat and then walks out to the beach. She then sees Matt in the water and joins him.

"Hey! You finally got up and out today." Matt says, "Yeah, I know. I was so tired today and don't know why." Says Moreen. They then stand in the water at chest level and watch as the sun descends on the horizon. When the sun was no longer visible, Matt and Moreen sit on the shoreline. They sat there for about an hour before walking back to the house. At the house, Moreen sits on the porch, while Matt goes inside and grabs some drinks for the two of them.

For several hours through the night, they sit on the porch drinking. The weather outside is very warm, but they have a nice and pleasant breeze in the atmosphere and there is not a cloud in the bright moonlit summer night sky. As it got later and later into the night, Matt got more drunk before finally going inside the house and dozing off to sleep.

It has now been 6 full weeks that Matt and Moreen have been stuck on this island, and back on the mainland, people are getting more worried about them both. As for Matt, his friends, co-workers, and bosses do not know what to think as they have had no contact with him. Moreen has her friends, and school officials at her university worried as she is supposed to begin classes in a couple weeks. There was a massive search that happens countrywide 2 weeks ago, but with no sight or leads, they called it off. They even interviewed the people on their plane which told then about the short unexpected layover, but everyone thought everyone was accounted for.

Ch 6. Weeks 7-9 on the island

Shortly after sunrise, they both awake, still feeling tired they lay there for moments resting. When they finally get out of bed, they first make themselves breakfast, and after it is maid, they take the food and some sodas out on the porch. The morning sun is shining bright as there is not a cloud in the sky, but it is not too hot because it is very windy this morning. As they sit outside for a few hours, they talk, mostly about what made them venture away from the plane that first day.

By noon, the wind had gone away, and it became scorching hot. With it being so hot, Matt and Moreen took a dip in the creek for a few hours. By the middle of the afternoon, the sky above became cloudy, signaling to them a storm was brewing. As clouds started to build up, they keep an eye on the sky as they swim in the middle of the creek. Soon they decide to go back up to the porch. As they get out of the water, it becomes very windy. Once on the porch, Moreen sits down while Matt goes inside the house and grabs some drinks to bring out. The rain starts coming down just as Matt comes out to the porch with drinks.

They sit there for hours watching the rain, getting drunk, and enjoying the wind. After the first 3 hours, the rain and wind become unbearable, and they both retreat inside. Feeling drunk and horny, they have sex and then pass out. However, their rest only lats for a couple hours, and right before the sun begins to set, they are awake and sitting back out on the porch.

As the sun is setting, they walk out to

the beach to catch a bit of the sunset. But before they leave the house and head to the beach, they load up on some drinks. They walk quickly to the beach and get into the ocean water just as the sun hits the water on the horizon. As the sun slowly drifts downward, they swim and watch it. After about an hour they sit on the shoreline and begin drinking. As the evening turns to night, the moon is shining brightly off the ocean water.

As Matt and Moreen continue to rest and drink on the shoreline, they start to make out and do some touching. Within moments they are both very turned on. So, they exit the water, walk up the few feet, and start having sex. As they sexually satisfy each other, nature is satisfying them too with a tad less humid night and a very present light breeze. After Matt and Moreen get each other off, they go for another swim in the ocean water.

As it becomes later into the night, they exit the water and walk back to the house. After getting back to the house, Matt and Moreen sit outside on the porch to enjoy more of the pleasant weather they are having and more drinks. As they sit there together for a couple hours, they have a pleasant conversation getting to know each other more. They talk about what Matt and Moreen each plan to do once they get back on the mainland.

As it is approaching midnight, they are both very drunk, and they go inside the house to lie down. Before dozing off to sleep, they are horny once again, and right after finishing each other off, Moreen falls right to sleep. Matt, however, just lays there still awake. After Matt lays in bed for an hour and cannot get to sleep, he goes out and takes a dip in the creek. By nearly 2 AM, Matt exits the water to go back inside. Once inside he stands in the kitchen and drinks two beers, and then he goes to lay back down in bed. Within a matter of a few moments, Matt finally falls asleep.

The next day Matt wakes up around mid-morning, and Moreen is still very sound asleep. After waking up, Matt lays in bed for almost an hour before finally getting up out of bed. He leisurely strolls into the kitchen has a soda and something to eat. After having a bite to eat to start the day, he decides to go on a hike through the island.

After hiking about 3 miles north, he looks down on the ground below and notices that the grass color shade of this one area is greener than most of the island. So, sitting on a fallen tree trunk, he begins trying to uproot the grass. After several moments he has the grass unrooted, and there is a passageway with a ladder going underground; he explores it.

As Matt climes down this ladder, he is going under the island and into the ocean in an enclosed tunnel. Once he gets to the bottom of the ladder, he is a half a mile deep into the sea. The tunnel is sounded by glass looking at the water and is lit up when there is good sunlight. Matt walks the tunnel for about 3 hours, and he has unknowingly walked 6 miles. The tunnel stretches all the way to a beach on the west coast of Florida, 400-miles away.

Meanwhile, back at home, Moreen has been awake for hours, and it is the midafternoon. She looked around for Matt for an hour after she got up, but gave up after no sign of him. Right now, as it's about 3 PM she is outside hanging out in the creek. It is a scorching hot day, with the sun shining very brightly as the sky is clear, and it is very humid. Back in the tunnel, Matt is taking a rest and sitting on the floor of the tunnel. He sits there for approximately 2 hours before getting up and starting the long walk back to the exit.

As the sun begins to set, it gets very windy out of nowhere. Moreen, still in the water, looks up at the sky, and clouds are rolling in and building up. After she sees that she knows a storm is coming. So, she exits the water and goes into the house. She looks for Matt again and even shouts out his name, "Matt! Matt! Matt!" Nothing, so she gets herself a drink out of the fridge and walks back outside. As she is sitting there on the porch, the wind is really intensifying, but to her, it still feels good. As it is pouring down Matt is exiting the tunnel and has a 3-mile walk back to the house. Back at home, Moreen is getting tired and about ready to head off to bed.

157

Walking alone in the middle of the night with rain pouring down is hard and miserable for Matt. There is also the element of the strong wind too that makes it unbearable. But he has no other choice than to mussel his way through the elements and make his way home. The 3-mile hike takes him close to 3 hours, because he walks slowly to avoid falling and because there is very little light from the night sky. About 20 minutes before he arrives at the house the rain stops, which is a relief. When Matt arrives at home it is about 1 AM. With Matt still being very wet from the rain, he goes inside to get a drink. With his drink, he goes out on the porch where he stands for 20 minutes to dry off. After he is good and dry, he goes to lay down in bed. Moments after his head hit's the pillow he falls sound asleep.

In the mid-morning Matt and Moreen, both awake around the same time. Before getting out of bed they have sex as Matt wakes up with morning wood. The sex is excellent for both and lasts for almost a half-hour. They then get out of bed and leisurely stroll to the kitchen to get something to eat. Over their meal, they talk. "Where were you yesterday? I didn't see you the entire day," said Moreen, "I got up very early and I went for a hike. I discovered a tunnel that goes down under the island and sits in the ocean. The tunnel stretches for miles, in fact, I do not know how far. I will show it to you tomorrow, but I need a day to rest. I hope I did not worry you that much. How was your day yesterday?" Matt replied, Moreen then responded, "My day was good. I just hung around here and did the usual. That is interesting, what you found. I cannot wait to see it for myself.

After sitting inside eating and talking for an hour they make their way outside and go for a dip into the creek. The temperature today was not as hot as usual, because the sky was very cloudy, so the sun was not beating directly down on them. There was also a pleasant breeze and the water was the perfect temp. Matt and Moreen stay in the creek for about an hour swimming until it starts to drizzle.

In the mid-afternoon as a rain shower blows through Matt and Moreen sit on the porch and enjoy some drinks. The rain shower only lasts about an hour and a half but leaves behind strong winds. As they continue to sit on the porch the wind feels amazing. Matt and Moreen sit there for a few hours and then after the rain stopped and the sky cleared up, they decided to go up to the cliff and watch the sunset.

The walk up to the cliff is about 1.75 miles from there house and they leave the house with a couple hours of daylight left. The walk through the island was a bit warm, but with the wind blowing through the air, there was a feeling of comfort. Matt and Moreen arrived at the cliff as they had 30 minutes before sunset. So, the sat with their bare asses in the sticky grass and their legs dangling over the ledge. After moments sitting there, Moreen starts rubbing Matts dick and it gets hard. With them, both aroused they have anal sex in the doggy style position as the sunsets. After they finish having sex both continue to sit on the cliff for a few hours more. With the moon well lighting the ocean and island Matt and Moreen jump off the cliff and into the ocean below.

Matt and Moreen then swim for about 3 miles around the perimeter of the island reaching their main beach. Before they exit the water at the main beach they sit on the shoreline and talk for a bit. "This, being on this island has been quite an adventure," Moreen says. "Yes, it has, and I am glad to share it with you. However, I cannot wait until we leave this island and get back to society," Matt responds, "Dido," says Moreen. With no drinks, they both walk back to the house. At the house, Moreen right away sits on the porch, while Matt goes inside and get some drinks to bring out for them. With the moon well lighting the island and the pleasant breeze they relax on the porch for hours drinking. After hours passing by sitting there on the porch getting drunk Matt and Moreen go lay down and right away dose off to sleep.

At around 2 AM Matt awakes after sleeping for only a couple hours. He lays there for a bit trying to fall right back to sleep. After he lays there for 30 minutes and does not, he gets out of bed and takes a few drinks out on the porch. He then sits there on the porch alone for about an hour and a half then goes back inside and falls asleep.

Moreen wakes up right after sunrise and with Matt still sound asleep, she climbs out of bed and makes herself something to eat. She then hangs out on the porch for a few hours. As hours pass Matt is still asleep so with Moreen being bored she walks alone out to the beach. Once on the beach, she lies on the warm sand and gets a nice tan. Meanwhile back at the house, Matt is just waking up. Matt then eats and goes out on the porch where he sits for about an hour.

As Moreen is at the beach it begins to rain. So, as it rain's she leaves the beach and begins walking back to the house. Matt sees her in the distance as she approaches and says, "You were at the beach." Moreen smirks as she walks up onto the porch. They then sit there for a few moments. As it continues to rain Matt walks off the porch and into it. He stands on a nice green grassy area under the rain trying to make his dick hard. Moreen watches for a few moments and then walks slowly over to him.

She then kneels next to him and grabs his dick.

Moreen strokes his dick for a little bit before putting it in her mouth and giving Matt a blowjob as it rains on them. Matt then lays down on the wet grass. Moreen hops on top of him pitting his dick into her pussy with her boob facing him so he can watch them bounce. After a few minutes in that position, they switch to doggy style where Matt put his dick into her butt. They then continue to have anal sex until they both cum. As they finish it is still raining so they go back on the porch to hang out and have more to drink.

The rain clears out as the sun sets behind the clouds and with the storm moving away both Matt and Moreen decide to go relax in the creek. As they jump in the water the night sky is cloud-free and the moon is shining and reflecting off the water. With the water soothing them and the breeze blowing above they swim around for a few hours.

By midnight Matt and Moreen are

feeling tired and exit the creek and go in the house. Before going off to bed they both have a drink standing inside and then lay down. Within moments of their heads hitting the pillow, they fall asleep. After a few passing hours, Matt awakes before daybreak. As he is still very tired he lies there in the hopes of falling back to sleep right away. After laying there for an hour with no luck of falling back to sleep, he quietly gets out of bed.

With Moreen asleep still, Matt leaves the house and walks back to the tunnel and enters it. With the rising of the sun, he can see his way around the tunnel and walks for 3 hours and goes 8 miles away from the entry. Back at the house, it is mid-morning and Moreen is just waking up. When she gets out of bed, she has something to eat before going out and jumping in the creek for a while. As she swims around in the water, she is looking around the landscape noticing that Matt is not around.

Matt walks a bit further and comes to a fork in the tunnel where it has 2 pathways. He is then unsure what to do and stands in one spot for a few moments. He then decides to walk back and go back to the island. With him feeling tired the walk back takes him way longer than usual.

As the sun begins to set Matt gets out of the tunnel and is very tired, so he lays down on the grass next to the entry point. Moreen gets is tired of hanging out by the house. So, she goes of a hike around the island, although it's getting dark. She hikes for about an hour as the sun is setting behind her and finds Matt laying on the grass. "What the hell are you doing?" Moreen asks, "I'm tired, and been in the tunnel all day," Matt replies. "so, this is where the tunnel is?" Moreen says as she goes into it to see for herself. As she goes down into it to look for herself there is not that much light because of the sunset. So, after taking just a little peek in it she gets out. Moreen then sits on the grass next to Matt and then after an hour, they both walk back to the house together.

Once at the house, Matt gets some drinks and goes to hang out on the porch and

Moreen sits there with him. "Were you in that tunnel all day?" Moreen asks, "Yes, I left right as the sun was rising. The tunnel goes for miles and miles and when the sun reflects well off the water you can see good down there." "How far do you think the tunnel goes?" asks Moreen, "I have no idea." After sitting on the porch for a few hours and have several drinks they go lay down around midnight. Before going to sleep they have sex, it lasts for 20 minutes and then they right away pass out.

Matt and Moreen wake up the following morning kind of early, about an hour after sunrise. Feeling rested they right away jump out of bed and go get a bite to eat to start the day. Right after eating they grab a cooler of drinks and take it with them out to the beach. When they arrive at the beach, they right away get into the water to cool off under the bright beaming hot sun, they swim in the water for a few hours, and then around noon they sit on the shoreline and start drinking. As Matt and Moreen sit there they see a boat in the distance. They continue to watch it for a while as it gets closer and closer to them.

The boat docks up on the beach about a half-mile from where they are sitting. Onboard is a group of teens 18-21. There are 5 of them however one of them is 16 but with his older 19-year-old sister. The other three are close friends to the sister one guy and 2 girls. One of the girls right away gets off the boat and goes to say hello to Matt and Moreen but is surprised when she approaches them, as they are naked. Matt and Moreen quickly explain that they have no clothes and tell her that they have been stuck on the island for quite some time. After the girl spends a few moments talking with them she goes back over to her friends.

The girl then goes back to her friends and tells them that Matt and Moreen are naked. They don't have clothes and she expresses her beliefs that she thinks these two are the people she's heard about on the news that others were looking for. Moreen and Matt then go back into the water and swim more after sitting on the shoreline for a few hours. Meanwhile, the people from the boat get off their boat and explore the island.

As the sun begins to set everyone gathered on the beach. The people from the boat join Matt and Moreen and sit in a group and watch the sunset. The boat people felt weird at first because Matt and Moreen were naked, but after an hour the weirdness went away. After sunset, the moon well lights up the island and they all sit there on the beach for a while drinking. As everyone is feeling good and drinking. As they drank more the three girls from the boat decide to get topless, witch makes the youngest guy there feel weird because he now must see his sister's boobs.

As the night continues everyone gets really drunk but soon it begins to rain. As the rain starts Matt and Moreen invite their new friends back to their house and as they all start to walk to the house it becomes very windy. They all walk back to the house and hang out on the porch drinking more and enjoying the breezy wind. After some passing time, the girls from the boat decide to join Matt and Moreen in being naked. So, as everyone sits on the porch the girls remove their bottoms too. As it is approaching midnight, it is still raining and very windy with nothing more to do they all take the party inside. Feeling aroused as everyone is naked Matt and Moreen start having sex with each other not caring about being watched. Shortly after them starting the others do too. When Matt and Moreen finish they go lay down alone while the others rest in other parts of the house.

The next morning Matt awakes as the sun is rising and feeling well-rested, he goes outside and jumps in the creek. He is out there alone as everyone else is still in the house sleeping. After an hour of swimming, he goes back to the house to get some food. As he stands eating in the house one of the girls from the boat wakes up and puts on some pants and hangs out with Matt. After Matt is done eating, he goes back out to the creek and gets back in the water. The girl follows him and removes her bottoms before jumping in the creek with Matt. Matt and the girl are out there alone for a couple hours while everyone else is still asleep in the house. Matt and the girl touch one another, and the girl ends up giving matt a hand job.

Everyone else awakes right before noon and go out and swim around in the creek. They all hang out and have fun until the middle of the afternoon. At around 4 that afternoon everyone walks back to the beach where the people from the boat say they must go to their boat to grab a few items. They make Matt and Moreen believe there not leaving but as soon as they all board the boat, they right away take off continue their journey of boating across the globe. As they pull away from the beach Matt and Moreen sit there on the shoreline and watch as they depart. However, they only make it to the other side of the island before their boat runs out of gas. Matt and Moreen start swimming around there in the ocean.

At around sunset, Matt and Moreen get out of the water and stand there on the sand watching the setting of the sun. While Moreen stands there, she feels horny and kneels on the warm sand and starts to give Matt head. Then Matt gets horny and lies down on the beach. With the sun halfway down on the horizon, Moreen sits on top of Matt putting his dick inside her pussy. After 5 minutes in that position they move to doggy style were Matt puts his dick into her ass. They then finish 5 minutes later and then go sit on the shoreline drinking and watching the remaining of the sunset.

About an hour a half after the sun is down, they go walk back to the house. During their walk, it is nice and breezy and the moon is well lighting the island. After getting back home Moreen is tired and goes to lay in bed while matt stays up for a little while sitting on the porch and having a few more drinks. When Matt goes to lie down in bed Moreen wants to have sex again. So, they do and then fall right to sleep after.

A bit after dawn the next day Matt and Moreen both awake. Moreen, feeling well-rested gets right out of bed while Matt still lays there alone for a while. After having something to eat, Moreen takes a walk through the island going back to the tunnel. With it being early in the morning and the sunlight well reflecting off the water she walks for 4 hours through the tunnel going a distance of 12 miles. Back at home, it is approaching noon, and Matt finally gets out of bed. He looks for Moreen for about an hour and with no sight of her gives up and goes alone out to the beach.

As Matt swims alone in the ocean he wonders where Moreen could be. Back in the tunnel Moreen sits on the floor of it and rests for about an hour before she gets up to start walking back. At about 3 in the afternoon, after swimming for a couple hours Matt sits on the shoreline and starts to drink some beer's that he has in the cooler out to the beach. At around sundown, Moreen exits the tunnel and walks out to the beach, where Matt is. She gets into the water to go for a nice swim as the sun is setting. Matt joins her and they stay swimming in the water for a couple hours. After the sun is down the moon well lights up the island. Matt and Moreen sit on the shoreline and begin drinking. They end up sitting there until they are completely drunk and walk completely out of the water and lie on the beach. As they lie on the beach, they have sex, and right after they finish, they pass out.

After sleeping for a few hours, just because they were drunk, Matt awakes just after midnight. Under the bright moonlit summer sky, he goes for another swim in the ocean. He swims for about 20 minutes and he decides to go on a walk around the beach. After walking for 3 hours he ends up on the opposite side of the island and sees the boat that he saw the other day. With the lights out on it and nobody in sight, he does not approach it. Matt then walks through the center of the island, through some wooded area, and arrives back on the main beach. The sun is rising and Moreen is still laying there sound asleep. Matt then walks alone back to the house and gets into bed and passes out.

About an hour after dawn, Moreen sleeping on the beach awakes. With no sight of Matt, she immediately walks back home. At home, she searches the house and finds Matt alone in bed sound asleep. With Moreen feeling well-rested she goes for a hike around the island and goes up to the cliff. She plans to stay the day there basking in the sun but after an hour she gets startled as she is joined by the teenage boy from the boat. "O my God! What the hell are you doing here? I thought you all left." Moreen says, "I'm just exploring the island. Our boat ran out of gas. Why are you always naked?" The boy responds. Moreen says "We lost all our clothes and being naked is freeing."

Moreen and the boy sit there alone together and after a bit he says, "I have never seen boobs in real life before," "Ok, do you like what you see? Want to touch?" Moreen replies. Then the boy starts touching her boobs and after moments gets naked himself. They then sit there for a little while and then after them getting bored they jump off the cliff and into the ocean. They swim to the closest beach which is a half-mile away. After arriving the boy gets embarrassed as everyone from the boat is sitting on the beach. Moreen quickly gets out of the water and rests on the beach while the boy still is in the water.

After an hour of the boy not moving an inch his sister yells "Are you going to join us or what?" he says nothing back and keeps swimming. Then the sister talks to Moreen: "We met at this cliff and swam to this beach. I dared him to do it naked, so he got naked." Moreen says, the sister responds, "I am his sister, so my brother is naked, dang, probably why he will not get out of the water." The sister then leaves the beach and walks into the middle of the island. Moments after she does the boy exits the water and Moreen grabs his hand and takes him back up to the cliff where the boy retrieves his clothes.

Back at the beach as the sun sets the sister rejoins her friends and parties with them and they decided to get naked. Meanwhile, after the boy retrieves his close Moreen walks him back to the beach and he gets a shock when everyone including his sister is chilling naked. The boy stands off to the side and thinks to himself for a second. With the thought of "What the hell" he joins everyone deciding not to be disturbed by seeing his sister naked. As the people from the boat and Moreen are parting on the beach, Matt is just waking up back at home.

Matt searches for Moreen around the inside and outside of the house. When he cannot find her, he gives up. He then sits out on the porch and drinks for a few hours. Then in the evening, he goes to the beach taking some drinks with him. With the sun already down, he walks with a cooler of drinks under a moonlit sky to the beach. Matt then sits on the shoreline alone drinking as the waves smash on him. After not seeing Moreen for 5 hours he wonders where she is and after a while chilling alone on the beach he goes for a long hike down the beach. At near midnight and after walking 2 and a half miles he finds Moreen parting with the people from the boat and joins in.

After everyone is there for a few hours and after getting really drunk they all have a big group sex orgy on the beach under the bright night sky. Matt got lucky and got to penetrate two of the girls from the boat, while Moreen helped the young teen boy lose his virginity. The beach orgy lasted for about an hour, and when everyone finished, they all went their separate ways. Matt and Moreen went in the warm ocean water and swam their way back to their main beach, while the others walked through the island back to their boat.

After Matt and Moreen arrived at the beach they sat on the shoreline and rested for a few moments before walking back to there house. By the time they arrive back at home it is a bit after 1 AM. Moreen, feeling tired goes right to bed and quickly falls asleep. Meanwhile, Matt chills out on the porch and drinks for about another hour before going to bed himself. Surprisingly, Matt drifts off to sleep right after laying down.

Very early in the morning as the sun is rising the genie appears to awake them and says "I have some news, you both will somehow get off the island before another month goes by. You can use the tunnel or wait for something to appear. However, I am here to offer one last tool or luxury. You can either have lights in the tunnel or entertainment in the house. As they have a minute to decide, Matt and Moreen quickly tell the genie lights in the tunnel. The genie grants it and then quickly vanishes. Feeling a bit tired they both lay back down. Matt falls right back to sleep but Moreen does not and after a half-hour of laying there she gets out of bed. She makes herself something to eat and then after eating she goes to relax in the creek for a bit. As she makes her way outside the sky is cloudy and it is extremely windy. After getting into the creek she gets out 20 minutes later as it begins to rain and the wind intensifies more. As she makes her way on to the porch, Matt, who just woke up a few moments ago is standing there. "Wow, this looks like it is going to be a really bad storm," Matt says. With nothing really to do they both go back inside the house.

As they sit together Moreen begins rubbing Matts dick and when it gets firm enough she repositions herself and begins sucking on it. Moreen gives Matt a nice long blowjob before sitting on his lap and putting it into her pussy. After a few moments in that position, they change to doggy style, and then to one more position before they both have an orgasm. After having sex, they both start drinking and they end up sitting in the house drinking most of the day. After a few passing hours, the storm comes to an end.

Once the storm ends Matt and Moreen go out on the porch to get some fresh air. The sun was still out but setting and the storm system left behind some strong gusts of wind. After sitting on the porch for a few moments Matt and Moreen decided to take a walk to the beach to watch what was left of the sunset. They got to the beach just as the sun was half-way into the horizon, it was a beautiful view. The temp outside felt amazing with the wind gusts as they sat on the damp sand near the water. However, they decided to stay out of the water due to the powerful waves left behind by the storm system. The sunset looked amazing on this night as they gazed at it and got their drink on and right after the sun disappeared the moon shined brightly on the island.

Matt and Moreen sit there relaxing on the beach for a few hours and at times gaze at the bright summer night sky. During there night at the beach, they have sex, and then at close to midnight, they start to head back to the house. When they arrive back at the house, they sit on the porch for about another hour. In their hour of sitting on the porch, they enjoy the soothing of the windy weather and each has a few more drinks. After an hour they both feel tired and go lay down quickly falling asleep.

Feeling rested Matt awakes within a few hours right before the sun rises and gets out of bed. Then with Moreen still asleep, he goes to grab something to eat and then leaves the house. He walks to the tunnel to explore more of it. He discovers that the floor of the tunnel is lit up and the lights have numbers. These numbers show how many miles they are away from a Florida beach, but Matt does not know that. Matt then walks through the tunnel for 3 hours and goes 15 miles, which is the longest he has ever walked. To rest, he sits down on the floor of the tunnel.

Meanwhile back at home, it is mid-morning and Moreen is just waking up. She goes to the kitchen and eats some food and as she is eating she thinks about going to explore the tunnel too. However, she does not walk to the tunnel right away. She first takes about an hour and chills in the creek. After getting in the water she swims for a bit and then sit's on the ledge thinking to herself and enjoys the sun. At about noon she begins her walk to the tunnel. Meanwhile, already inside the tunnel Matt gets back up and resumes walking further. By the time Moreen enters the tunnel, Matt is 16.5 miles away from the entrance point.

Matt and Moreen both keep walking through the tunnel for the next couple of hours. However, after a couple hours Matt stops and rests again at the 21-mile mark, while Moreen keeps walking as shes at only the 11-mile mark. Matt sits there for about an hour before standing up and walking the long walk back to the tunnel entry point. After walking for an hour, he meets Moreen at the 16-mile mark. "Moreen! What are you doing?" "Exploring the tunnel, like you. Why, do you think you're the only one that should explore this tunnel?" Moreen responds. Matt has no response to that and says, "I'm going home." Matt continues to walk towards the exit of the tunnel as Moreen walks more further into the tunnel

When Matt finally exits the tunnel, the sun is setting. With the sun setting, he hurries to the cliff and stands there watching the sunset until the sun is gone. As the sun is down the moon lights up the island and Matt jumps off the cliff into the ocean. Matt then swims for about 3 miles back to the main beach and sits on the shoreline for a bit. Meanwhile, back in the tunnel Moreen has walked 17 miles and is 2 miles away from the entrance point. The new lights in the tunnel make the tunnel look cool as the ocean surrounding the tunnel is dark. At around midnight Matt is back at the house sitting on the porch having a few drinks while Moreen is just arriving home.

Moreen right away goes inside to get something to eat and drink then she joins Matt sitting on the porch. They then sit there for a couple hours getting drunk together before going to bed. When they first lie down in bed they have sex, and right after they finish the pass out and sleep sound the rest of the night.

After sleeping for almost 7 hours Matt and Moreen awake close to 11 AM. When they awake they feel well-rested and right away get out of bed. They first go get something to eat and relax around the house for a little bit.

A bit after noon time they get a cooler, fill it with drinks, and walk out to the beach. However, instead of getting into the water where they normally do, they walk down the beach 2 miles to the area where everyone was at the other night. By 2 PM they arrive at that beach and the people from the boat are not there yet. So, Matt and Moreen just get in the water and go for a nice swim. Although it was cloudy during there walk there, once they get into the water there was not a cloud in the sky and the sun is beaming down on them.

As they swim for an hour the people from the boat emerge from the wooded area and make their way out on the beach. Matt and Moreen are instantly spotted and one of the people from the boat says "Hey! What are you guys doing on this side? You are far from your beach." "We just wanted to hang out with you all. Hope you do not mind," Moreen replies back. The people from the boat stand there on the beach and think about it for a moment, they then respond "You know what... Shure why not." Then everyone makes there way into the water. Matt and Moreen only swim around for another 20 minutes and then sit on the shoreline and start drinking.

While the others stay out in the water and swim for another hour.

At around sunset, they are all sitting on the beach drinking and watching the sunset. They also start to talk more to get to know each other. "Where are all of you from?" Matt asks, "We are from a city in the southeast corner of Georgia. What about you two?" The oldest one responds, Matt says "Well she is from Nevada and I'm from New York City." Matt continues to say, "We met on this flight going from Vegas to South Florida. I was on a 2-month vacation from work and I'm an investor advisor." They all found is job interesting and continued to talk and drink.

Quickly after the sun was down it became windy, but not too windy and it was pleasant. The moon well lighted up the island and they all went back in the water for another swim. Everyone swam for about an hour and when they all exited the water Matt and Moreen began to walk back home.

Matt and Moreen returned home about an hour before midnight. After arriving home Moreen went straight to bed while Matt stayed up for another couple of hours relaxing on the porch and drinking a few more cold alcoholic beverages. As he sat on the porch drinking the wind soothed him and made him feel delighted. At around 1 in the morning, Matt went inside and to bed. As he got situated in bed Moreen awoke and felt horny. So, they had sex and it lasted a good 10 minutes and after they finished, they both passed out almost instantly.

After sleeping for approximately 6 and a half hours, Matt and Moreen both awake at around 11 that morning. After waking up they hop right out of bed and get there grub on to begin the day. After having brunch they both go sit out on the porch. The sky above them is cloudy and there are very powerful wind gusts. After being outside for only 20 minutes it begins to pour down. However, they continue to sit there for about an hour. They are finally forced to go back inside when the wind gets so strong that it's causing the rain to hit them in the face.

With nothing more to do, they go back inside, and with them being bored they make each other get aroused. They then have an hour-long sex episode in every possible position known to man. Moreen cums about 4 times while Matt cums twice, after the first time he powers through to keep an erection to keep going. After they're done they stay seated inside and start drinking. As they sit inside for a few hours they notice the noises of the pouring rain have ceased so in the late afternoon they go back out to the porch.

The sky above has cleared up a bit, but it is still raining lightly, and the wind was still intense. However, the wind feels perfect on their naked bodied as they sat on the porch to enjoy the feeling and some cold drinks for a couple hours. The rain stopped as the sun was just beginning to set and with it no longer raining Matt and Moreen walked out to the beach. They took drinks with them out to the beach and sat on the wet sand to watch the sunset. There was not a cloud in the sky. After the sun was down they remained on the beach enjoying the windy weather and some cold drinks.

The night sky over the island was bright and had some nice-looking views of stars. Moreen gazed at the nighttime sky in infatuation for some time. As they sat on the beach later into the night the waves of the ocean water calmed down and Matt went for a swim. Near midnight Matt and Moreen left the beach and went back to there house. Once at the house they both spent another few hours drinking on the porch before going to bed.

Matt was last to get in bed and fall asleep at close to 2 AM but he only slept for a few hours getting back up right before dawn. When he awoke, he felt well rested and decided to start his day early. With Moreen still sound asleep Matt left out of the house and went for another exploration in the tunnel. But when he first got to the entrance point, he sat on the island ground with his legs dangling into the staircase to rest his body. He sat in that position for an hour and then made his way down into the tunnel.

After Matt enters the tunnel, he walks for 3 hours straight going 12 miles. He then rests for 30 minutes sitting on the floor of the tunnel. As he sits there, he sees a school of fish and a shark. The shark sees him and tries to get at him but the glass surrounding the tunnel is strong enough to keep the glass intact. Matt then gets up from the floor and walks another 2 hours going 28 miles total in the tunnel. Meanwhile, back on the island and at home it is just after 12 noon and Moreen is just waking up.

As Moreen awakes in the bed alone she right away jumps up and makes herself some grub. After having a meal, she goes to sit on the porch. The sky is clear, the sun is beaming down, and there is really no smoothness of wind. After getting very hot just by sitting on the porch for 10 minutes, she walks to the shortest body of water from the house, the creek. After an hour swimming around she realizes that Matt is nowhere around the house's vicinity. She then spends time thinking to herself as she is still in the water.

As it becomes later in the afternoon, Matt is still in the tunnel and he has walked 33 miles deep into it. While Moreen is still back on the island chilling out in the creek. At around sunset, Moreen walks alone through the island, and up to the cliff. When she arrives at the cliff, she sees the teenage boy again from the boat sitting naked on the ledge alone and joins him. The two of them watch the sunset together. As they sit there and watch the sunset Moreen allows the boy to touch her. Meanwhile, Matt is in the tunnel still under the island making his way towards the exit point.

After the sun is down the moon in the summer night sky lights up the island. Moreen and the teenage boy walk together from the cliff to a beach close by. On the beach, they still find themselves alone and begin to talk about each other to one another, "Why are you guys still here and where are all your friends." "Everyone is back near the boat and our boat ran out of gas. We have friends coming to help us out, but it will be days before they arrive." The boy says as he sits there with Moreen.

Miles away Matt has returned home after walking all day through the tunnel. With Matt feeling so tired he went straight to bed while Moreen was still out on the island. As it got closer to midnight Moreen left the boy with a goodnight kiss and began to make her way home. She swam in the warm ocean water down the beach under the bright moonlit sky for about 2 miles and then walked the other mile back to her main beach.

Meanwhile, it's about 1 AM and after sleeping for a couple hours Matt awakes. With Moreen still not back home yet Matt gets out of bed, gets some cold beers out the fridge, and goes to sit on the porch. After an hour of Matt sitting there alone Moreen appears and joins Matt; "Hello, where were you?" Matt asks, "I could ask you the same. But whatever." Moreen replies. Matt has nothing more to say after that and they just sit there on the porch together enjoying each other's company. After an hour as it's approaching 3 AM they both make their way to bed where they pleasure each other for a bit before dozing off to sleep.

After them both resting soundly for a solid 6 hours they both awake feeling rested just a couple hours before noon. After eating and getting themselves ready for the day they both decide to spend a beach day together just the two of them. So, as it approaches the early to mid-afternoon they go out to the beach with a cooler full of drinks.

Meanwhile, on a beach on the other side of the island, the people and their boat are still stuck but they are only hours from getting help, and as they wait for help, they are swimming and parting too.

As Matt and Moreen swim in the ocean water the air temperature around them is unusually pleasant, but the sky above them is cloudy. As Matt and Moreen swim around they continue to keep an eye on the sky. At one point through the afternoon the clouds in the sky looked so bad as if it would storm for hours but they only got a quick summertime shower and that was it. Matt and Moreen exited the water right after the rain shower and sat on the beach to sunbathed.

After a few passing hours basking in the sun, Matt and Moreen take another dip into the water as the sun is creeping down the horizon. After swimming for an hour they sit in the water on the shoreline enjoying some drinks and watching a pleasant sunset in a cloud-free sky. An hour after the sun is down the moon rises and fully lights up the summer night sky. Matt and Moreen sit there on the shoreline for a little while longer before walking back home.

It's only about 10 PM once they arrive back at home and the temperature outside is wonderful. So, they sit out on the porch and drink for a few hours. However, as they are relaxing and feeling good, a night storm rolls in, and it becomes very intense quickly. So, they go inside and off to bed. Once in bed, with them both being very drunk, they fall asleep quickly and sleep soundly through the entire night.

After 6 hours it is right before sunrise and Matt feels well-rested as he awakes. As Moreen is still asleep he walks to the other end of the island to watch the sunrise. As it becomes mid-morning, Matt makes his way back home and as he does a storm is rolling in. as he approaches the porch Moreen is sitting there and he says "Well we can't do shit now," and Matt joins her sitting on the porch watching the rain pour down. They sit there for an hour and after thinking the downpour would not stop soon, they begin day drinking.

Within a few hours, the wind pushed the rain up on to the porch, and is was hitting them in there faces. So, they went inside for a few hours, fucked, and drank. Near the middle of the afternoon the sky cleared up and Matt and Moreen went out to the beach. With the storm leaving behind some strong waves they did not go into the water. However, they sat in the sand where they could still get a bit wet.

Matt and Moreen sat there in that spot watching the sunset and it was a pleasant view. After some passing hours getting drunk and well after nightfall the two walk back home. When they arrive back at home it is not even midnight. So, they both decide to take a dip in the creek for an hour or so. They then sit in the creek for a few hours and then make there way back to the house. With Moreen feeling tired she goes straight in the house and to bed while Matt hangs out on the porch for a couple more hours, enjoying the wind on his body. By 2 AM. And being totally blotto, Matt goes inside and lays in bed where he falls fast asleep.

In the early morning that next day Matt and Moreen both awake feeling well-rested. After getting some grub to start the day, they chill out for a few hours in the house. By about noon they both go sit outside on the porch and Matt begins day drinking. The sky above them is cloudy and it is very windy, but they continue to sit on the porch enjoying the wind.

After an hour, and it not storming yet, Matt and Moreen take a dip in the creek. They are in the water for only an hour before the storm rolls in. with it pouring down they exit the water and move, at a quick pace to the porch. Moreen quickly dries herself off and goes inside to get drinks for her and Matt, while Matt airdries on the porch. As the storm is passing, they have hot sex on the porch doing many positions and lasting for almost an hour.

As it gets later into the afternoon, the storm keeps getting more intense. With nothing else really to do, Matt and Moreen go lay down and doze off to sleep. They are asleep for a few hours and wake back up around mid-evening as the sun is nearly set. It has stopped storming but is windy as hell. Despite how windy it is, Matt and Moreen take a walkout to the beach where they chill out for a while.

After a few hours of them sitting on the beach drinking, they have sex and it lasts for a while. The sex starts as they are knee-deep into the water and then moves onto the damp sand. After they both have a rocking orgasm they continue to sit on the beach and have more to drink. In the wee morning hours, as they are drunk, they leave the beach and walk back to the house. When they arrive, Moreen right away goes in and gets in bed while Matt sits outside on the porch for a while longer. As it approaches about 2 AM Matt takes a dip in the creek for like 20 minutes and then goes inside and lays down. As he's getting into bed Moreen awakes and starts to cuddle with Matt. The cuddling turns into massaging private areas and they have sex. After both having a great orgasm, they both quickly dose off to sleep.

Matt awakes after only sleeping a couple hours. So, with him feeling exhausted still, he lies there for a bit and eventually falls back to sleep. After a few more hours and right after sunrise they both awake and both start there day by mutually masturbating together in bed. Right after they both finish, they go get some morning grub and sit on the porch. After they sit there for an hour they both go together for a walk to the tunnel to explore it further. After entering the tunnel they walk for 4 hours straight going a distance of 30 miles.

At that point, they sit on the floor of the tunnel to rest for about an hour before getting back up. They then walk for another couple of hours going an additional 9 and a half miles.

that point they see something that stays "FL-1015mi". As they are both exhausted the get-up and begin the long walk to the entrance of the tunnel. On there way back, at the halfway point, they take a 30-minute rest, before they walk the other half. By the time they exit the tunnel, it is in the early evening hours. With a couple hours of daylight left.

Matt and Moreen walk to the beach, passing the house along the way. When they reach the house they relax at home for a few moments to rest their legs and then grab some drinks and snack food. Whit them still feeling worn out from the day they've had thus far it takes them an hour to get to the beach. Right before the sun begins to set they sit on the beach and begin drinking. As they sit there they are smoothened by a steady breeze of wind.

After the sun sets the moon well lights up the sky and Matt and Moreen go for a dip in the ocean. They swim around for nearly an hour then spend some time sitting on the shoreline. They spend about 2 hours sitting there and enjoying drinks, but when they run out of drinks they quickly make there way back to the house where they drank more.

As it becomes midnight Moreen is very tired and goes to lie down while Matt stays out on the porch for a few more hours and keeps drinking. After some passing hours, Matt goes off to bed as he is drunk. As he climbed into bed Moreen awakes and Matt cuddled her with his hand cupping her boob as he falls asleep.

After 6 hours at about 8, the next morning Matt and Moreen get up. They have a meal to start there day and then go relax on the porch. In the morning hours the sky above them was clear but as it, because noontime the sky became cloudy like a storm was coming. They wanted to have a productive day, so with the storm coming, they choose to go explore the tunnel some more.

As Moreen starts walking towards the tunnel Matt goes in the house to grab some drinks to take with them and catches up to

Moreen. It begins pouring down rain as soon as they enter the tunnel. After entering they walk for 2 hours non stop going a distance of 13 miles. Then they sit down on the floor of the tunnel to rest. They rest for an hour and each have a couple of drinks. After resting they walk for another 3 straight hours going 14 more miles in the tunnel and then rest as they are 27 miles away from the entrance of the tunnel.

They are getting tired and know it's getting late so they rest for about 2 and a half hours before starting the long walk to exit the tunnel. It takes them 6 hours to walk back and exit the tunnel and at the time they exit it's near midnight. After exiting the tunnel they lay down right beside the entrance to it, on the wet grass on the island.

Moreen and Matt both dose off right next to the tunnel's entrance, but they awake after a few short hours. When they awake they immediately walk back to the house. After they arrive at the house they right away go inside and go to bed and sleep soundly for the next 9 hours. At around 3 the next afternoon Matt and Moreen both get up. They have lunch and then load up a cooler to take to the beach. It is hot and humid outside and the sky is clear. With the sun beaming down and it not being that windy, they start to sweat a lot almost instantly after they walk out of the house.

Once Matt and Moreen arrived at the beach, they put the cooler on the sand and get into the water. They spend close to 2 hours swimming around to keep themselves cool. When they get tired of swimming they sit on the shoreline with half of their bodies still in the water and start drinking. They sit there for hours and watch the wonderful sunset. After the sun was down, it got cooled to a comfortable temperature. The bright moon lights up the island and water as they swam around near the shoreline. After a few hours sitting on the shoreline and drinking, they moved up on the sand and out of the water and have sex. The sex is very powerful and intense as they start out with oral and then move to vaginal and anal. Moreen has 4 orgasm while

Matt had 1 when he explodes a big load inside her ass. After the hour-long sex, they lay in the sand for 15 minutes to regain their energy.

They go in the water for another dip and to get the sand off them. After Matt and Moreen rinse off they start to make their way back home. It's close to midnight when they reach home but they are not ready for bed. They spend another few hours getting drunk and sitting on the porch enjoying the nighttime weather. There is a nice breeze from the wind that starts in the late night when they are sitting out there and it really soothes them for a good while. After a few hours with then being drunk, they make their way to bed where they dose off to sleep almost instantly.

In the mid-morning Matt and Moreen awake. However, with the many long days, they have recently had they are still feeling tired. They lay there for about an hour before getting out of bed to do anything. After slowly sagging out of bed at around noon they get themselves something to eat and spend time eating and relaxing in the house. "I liked spending time together with you but I really hope that we get off the island soon and get back to our lives." As they sit there, it starts to rain and it becomes more breezy. However, the rain only lasts for about 35 minutes and there is much more of the sunset to see. So, they walk out to the beach and watch the remaining of the sunset.

Matt and Moreen sit on the beach for a few hours and then right before midnight they start walking back home. When they arrive home they both right away go inside and off to bed. They sleep sound the whole night and by 10 AM the next morning they awake feeling well-rested. Moreen right away gets up, starts her day, and leaves the house while Matt still spends some time laying in bed. Moreen takes a walk around the island for a while. While Matt stays around the house and spends the day drinking.

At dusk, Moreen sits on the cliff of the island and watches the nice sunset. After the sun goes down she jumps into the ocean and swims for a while and halfway around the island. Back at home, Matt has fallen asleep out on the porch due to how drunk it got. It begins to rain as Moreen walks out of the water and onto the beach 2 miles away from the house.

The rain feels good to Moreen and it is just a rain shower, no thunder or lightning. She gets back home close to midnight and sees Matt passed out on the porch but she doesn't bother him and goes straight into the house, where she has something to eat and goes to bed. Matt wakes up on the porch at 2 AM, and with very little energy he stumbles in the house and lays in bed next to Moreen. After a few hours, Matt awakes and stays inside for a while

Hours after chilling inside Matt takes some drinks and goes out and sits on the porch. There is a heavy but nice breeze blowing, and the sky above is partly cloudy. As he sits there, Moreen goes into the creek by the house and swims around for a while. After a couple hours of Matt sitting on the porch and drinking, he begins to pleasure himself as the weather and the atmosphere turned him on. Seconds before he cums Moreen approaches on the porch and sits beside him. Matt then shoots his cum on her breast and Moreen just let it sit until it dries and she touches herself Whit Mat running low on beer in the cooler outside he goes inside to get more and then continues to sit on the porch and drink. Hours later, near sunset, it begins to rain and Moreen goes to bed. Matt continues to sit out there and he gets so drunk to where he falls asleep sitting on the porch.

Matt awakes about an hour later and finds himself out on the porch, he then goes inside, climbs into bed, and falls right back to sleep almost instantly. After a few passing hours and right after sunrise Matt and Moreen wake up. They right away get themselves something to eat and talk about what to do for the day. After discussing what to do, they decide to go explore the tunnel more and walk deeper into it than ever before.

Matt and Moreen leave the house around 9 and walk to the tunnel. Once they get into it they walk for a while and go 20 miles deep. They then sit and rest for a half-hour before walking another 15 miles. They then come to an intersection with one path going north and then the main path continuing east. They sit there and rest for an hour. Matt points to the north path and says "That could be going up into Mississippi wich is probably 125 miles. While continuing east we are about 200 miles from the west coast of Florida." "How do you know?" asks Moreen, Matt responds "educated guess.' (Matt's guess is in fact 100 percent right).

They have sex in the tunnel witch is something they have never done before and it feels liberating and great to both of them. The sex lasts for an hour and ends when they both have a powerful orgasm while Matt is inside of Moreen. They lay there on the floor of the tunnel for nearly another half-hour before rising to their feet and beginning the 35-mile walk back to exit the tunnel. The walk takes 8 hours and when they exit the tunnel the sun was already down and the island is in the middle of a tropical storm.

So, with it storming they climb back into the tunnel where they end up staying the night. Due to how exhausted they are they both right away fall asleep. Matt awakes after only an hour and a half and climbs up to the island to check the conditions. The storm had blown over and he goes back into the tunnel to tell Moreen to get up as it is good for them to walk home. It takes some time, but Moreen Finally awakes and Matt and Moreen walk home. As soon as they arrive home Moreen goes to bed while Matt sits outside for a few hours and drinks.

As Matt sits on the porch drinking in the middle of the night he gets soothed by the nice breeze in the air and the porch is well lit up by the moon. Matt has about 6 drinks over 2 hours and at nearly 3 in the morning he finally goes to bed himself. After 6 hours they both awake in the mid-morning feeling well-rested. They walk out on the porch after having some breakfast and the sky above is covered in clouds and it begins to rain as soon as they sit on the porch.

Even though it's raining outside Matt and Moreen sit on the porch to enjoy the cool outside air and begin day drinking. The sound and sight of the rain is enjoyable to them both as they get drunk. In the middle of the afternoon after being on the porch for a few hours the rain subsides and Matt and Moreen went to jump in the creek that is near the house.

They swim around in it for a few hours and then go to the beach around sunset.   As they load up a cooler with drinks and begin to walk out to the beach. It begins raining again and they get upset as they turn around and go back on the porch. With the sky being mostly clear they expect the rain to blow by quickly, it does and they walk out to the beach. They both spend a few hours on the beach, get a drunk, and have excellent sex.

At near midnight, after being very drunk they leave the beach and walk back to the house. When they get home they both go straight to bed as they are drunk and tired. Before drifting off to sleep they have hot drunken sex together and shortly after they finish Moreen falls to sleep very quickly while Matt lays there for a while before falling asleep himself.

After sleeping for about 10 hours Matt and Moreen wake up in the mid-afternoon. They eat a quick lunch and then go sit outside on the porch. They are surprised to see how heavily it is raining because they did not hear the rain when they were inside. However, they sit on the porch for a few hours and Matt starts day drinking. After the first hour sitting on the porch, the rain hasn't slowed down and the winds got stronger and more intense. By then they were in the middle of a tropical storm and went inside do to how powerful the winds were. They both stay inside for most of the day with how unsafe the conditions are

Back inside Matt continues to drink and Moreen also drinks a bit. After serval hours have gone by, and as its near sunset the rain stopped but the winds were still very strong. They wanted to walk up to the cliff of the island, were Matt had not been for a while. So they stand outside to feel the conditions. Due to how intense the wind was they chose not to go but they sat outside on the porch for a few hours. After sunset, the island became very dark, as the moon wasn't shining as bright tonight, so with nothing really to do and with the low light, they go inside very early and go to bed. Due to how early it was when they went to bed Matt awoke after a few short hours.

It was about midnight when Matt awoke. He laid there in bed for a little more than an hour next to Moreen to try and fall back to sleep. After almost an hour and a half, Matt gets out of bed and goes on the porch to start drinking more. He spends about 3 hours having 6 drinks and after he gets back in bed. Soon after he laid down he ends up falling sound asleep and sleeps the rest of the night.

The next morning at around 9 both Matt and Moreen got up. They made themselves a big breakfast and spent about 2 hours eating and talking. "Do you feel like being on this island taught you something?" Matt asks Moreen. "yes it did, I learned how to survive in the wilderness and to survive without technology and media. Being butt naked all the time is nice, and I have grown to like it witch is, something I never was sure about." During the afternoon and late into the night, they hangout on the beach. By 11 that night after spending 7 hours at the beach and drinking the whole time, they walk back to the house and immediately lie in bed. Moreen falls asleep right away while Matt lays there for 45 minutes before falling asleep himself.

Matt and Moreen both slept for a straight 13 hours and at around noon, on their 61st day on the island. They are getting bored after 2 months of being stuck, and they are tired, repeating the same routine over and over. However, they only have about nine more days left there, but they don't know that. As they have lunch, They chat a little. After some passing hours, Matt goes out on the porch and relaxes by himself while Moreen decides to spend the day resting in bed. Later that night, Moreen joins Matt on The porch, and they both start drinking a lot.

As they sit there, the wind is blowing pleasantly, and it is drizzling. After a few drinks in them, they start playing sexually with themselves and each other as they sit there. It lasts for about 2 hours on and off. They were At

209

around midnight when the rain stopped, they went out to the beach and did an all-nighter there. Were they swam, drank, and sexually played more. With the bright moon reflecting off the water, they could see well, and the view looked nice. As the sun started rising, they were in the water swimming and watching it grow from behind the trees. After being up all night at the beach, Matt and Moreen both walk home at about 10 in the morning. Moreen goes straight to bed while Matt sits on the porch having a few more drinks before going to bed himself at around noon. They both sleep the rest of the day and well into the middle of that following night.

Ch 7, the last week on the island

After being in bed and sleeping for nearly 17 hours they awake together at around noon on the first day of their last week on the island. They have a big brunch and go chill out together on the porch for a couple hours. Matt begins day drinking as they sit there on the porch and then in the late afternoon, they load up a cooler with drinks and go out to the beach. They arrive at the beach with hours before sundown. It is very hot, so, they right away jump in the water and swim around for a while. As the sun begins to set they sit on the shoreline with the water up to their hip and have a few drinks. The setting of the sun looks amazing and drops the temperature and brings along a nice breeze.

With a bit of sunlight left Matt and Moreen get touchy and scoot up out of the water and have sex. It lasts a bit over an hour as they do all positions many times and both cum a few times. After they finish they go back in the water and swim around under a dim summer night sky. After swimming for a while they sit back on the shoreline and finish off the last of the few drinks they have in there cooler.

As it approaches midnight Matt and moreen spend a while out there watching the waves crash up on shore, the view is nice but they are very drunk and have no choice but to sit in that same spot for a while until they sober up. However, there is a chill in the air. It is enjoyable, but it gets to be too much. So, as soon as they feel well enough they both leave and walk back to the house. Because they walked carefully it took about 40 minutes. As they are both very exhausted, they enter their cabin and go right to sleep.

Early in the morning, at about 9 AM, feeling rested they right away jump out of bed. Matt and Moreen then mosey into the kitchen and have some food to start the day. Then after eating they spend a couple hours inside talking to one another about random things that came to mind. Then close to noontime they start relaxing on the porch. After sitting out there enjoying themselves for nearly an hour and a half. Matt and Moreen both started day drinking. By 3 that afternoon they decide to go out to the beach. So, Matt loads up a bunch of drinks and then they walk to the beach. By the time they reach the beach they are sweaty due to how hot and humid it is. So, they set the cooler down on the sand for a bit and right away jump into the water. Matt and Moreen then spend a couple of hours swimming around, then as the sun begins to set they sit on the shoreline and resume drinking.

After the sun is completely down, it becomes dark as the sky above them is very cloudy and hiding the moon. Within an hour later light rain begins to fall on them. But, with it only being rain and no other elements they sit there and continue to drink on the shoreline. Within another passing hour, the rain totally stops and the moon comes out to shine on the beach. Therefore, Matt and Moreen go for another swim.

As it gets into the middle of the night, and with nothing left in there cooler, Matt and Moreen start making there way back to the house. As they walk back to the house they spot a box, but there's no note. So, they think nothing of it and go to the house for the night. When they arrive on the porch, it's not long after midnight, however they are both tired and go lie down in bed. Moreen falls right to sleep almost instantly, while Matt lays there for a bit and cannot seem to get himself to sleep.

After nearly an hour and a half of Matt laying there, he gets out of bed realizing he's not tired yet. He then grabs a couple of drinks and chills out on the porch. Matt sits on the porch for a few hours drinking a bit more, and then after 3 hours and feeling good and drunk he goes back to lie down in bed. Matt gets into bed very carefully, trying not to wake up Moreen and he falls right to sleep.

The next morning at 9 AM Matt and Moreen both awake. Feeling well-rested and a bit horny, they have sex, and then once they are finished they get out of bed and go grab something to eat. They spend all morning inside and at around noon Matt goes to sit on the porch while Moreen feels like being lazy and lays down for a couple hours. After Matt sits on the porch for about 30 minutes he begins day drinking. As he sits there the temperature outside is warm, but not hot and it's a bit humid. At around 3 that afternoon Moreen gets back up and joins Matt on the porch and drinks with him. As they sit there for a while they both begin touching on each outer and they get turned on and end up doing more. They do it right there on the porch and when they are done they go take a swim in the creek. They stay in the creek for only an hour and when they notice the sun was beginning to set they load up the cooler with drinks and start walking to the beach.

As Matt and Moreen walk to the beach the noticed that box again and they approached it trying to figure out why it was there. They opened it up and saw a note inside. The note told them that they only had days before they are rescued. So, stuff will disappear. The note concludes by telling them they have 2 hours from the time they read this note to put as many food items and drinks into the box. So, they right away empty there cooler and add the drinks to the box, then they run back into the house to get more to transfer to the box. By 90 minutes there box is full so they close the lid on it. They then reload there cooler and make there way to the beach. They get to the beach right as the sun is hitting the water and setting on the horizon. They stay out there on the beach well into the night and continue to drink. At about midnight they start walking home. However, when they get there the house is not their anymore but a nice big tent is.

Matt and Moreen spend a while just staring at the tent in disbelief. However, after the initial shock, they accept it and go lie down in the tent. As they try to fall asleep they snuggle up together, and that turns them on. So, they end up having some good hot sex before falling to sleep. When they do fall asleep it's about 3 AM.

Matt can't sleep and after only an hour he awakes. With Moreen still asleep he walks back over to the tunnels entrance point, but when he gets there the entrance is no longer accessible. Matt then stands there in disbelief and hunts around for a little bit seeing if the entry point is relocated. However, after a half an hour he relies it's gone for good and goes back to the tent where he lies back down.

In the early morning, a couple hours after sunrise Matt and Moreen awake. However, felling a bit tired they lie there for about 20 more minutes. Once fully awake the rise and walk out of the tent, they remember that the house they were living in didn't exist anymore and was converted to a tent. After a couple hours, as it was still morning and not too hot, they decided to move the tent from the middle of the island to the beach. The move took them a few hours to complete due to the size of the tent, some belongings, and the distance that everything had to go.

By noontime, everything was moved out to the beach and Matt and Moreen were both exhausted. They laid down in their tent for a few hours and then Matt got up. He went to the box took out a few drinks and start day drinking on the nice white sand. The temp was nice and it was breezy, witch felt good on his naked body and the sun didn't shine too bright, because of how cloudy it was. However, it felt comfortable and they enjoyed there afternoon.

As the sun started to set they started to swim around in the ocean. When the sun touched the horizon, Matt and Moreen stopped swimming and sat on the shoreline to gaze at the sunset. Matt and Moreen both drank more as they sat there in the shoreline of the ocean and watched the sunset. After the sun was completely down, the moon shined bright on the island and they went for another swim. They swam for almost 2 hours and then exited the water and sat on the sand near there tent and had a bit more to drink. After a few more passing hours, they got tired and went in their tent where they finally dozed off to sleep.

The next morning right as the sun is rising both Matt and Moreen awake. They right away go over to the box to grab some food to eat, and afterward, they take a blanket from the tent and lie out on the sand for several hours. In the early afternoon, it started to rain. So, Matt and Moreen took a little nap for about an hour and a half, by that time the rain had stopped but left behind a pleasant breeze that lasted the rest of the day.

The sunset was a nice view to both Matt and Moreen as they sat on the shoreline enjoying some drinks and that breeze. After the sun was completely down, they had the moon that brightly lighted up the island. So, as the moon shined brightly Matt and Moreen took a dip into the ocean where they swam around for a while. After a few hours of swimming and with it getting later into the night, they start to hang and drink close by the tent. With a thought that they would be up for a while, Matt started a fire to give them extra light.

With the fire started Matt and Moreen go back into the ocean for one last quick dip.

After spending only 15 minutes in the water they exit and sit on the beach and resume drinking. 3 hours later, by midnight, Matt has had 13 beers and Moreen has had 9. With them both being totally drunk, they pass out on the blanket outside of the tent. At around midnight after they are both drunk they go into their tent and right away go to sleep.

Matt only sleeps for 2 hours and awakes up wide awake in the middle of the night. After awaking he goes outside of the tent and has a few more drinks. At 3 AM it's kind of warm but there is a nice breeze and Matt goes for a dip under the bright summer night sky. By dawn, Matt lays back down in the tent and sleeps some more.

The next morning in the mid-morning Matt and Moreen both awake. Feeling well-rested only Moreen jumps out of the tent and grabs something to eat, while Matt continues to lie in the tent and gets another few hours of rest. By noon Matt reawakes and gets out of the tent. He doesn't see Moreen as she is hiking the island and going to chill out on the cliff. So,

Matt makes himself a sandwich and just hangs out on the beach for the rest of the day.

Moreen is on the cliff enjoying the scenery and a few drinks. To Moreen, the cliff feels a bit cooler than being on the flat island land and there is a pleasant breeze blowing the entire afternoon. Back at the beach, near the tent, Matt is enjoying the breeze too and the sky is partly cloudy witch is shading the sun. After a few hours as the sun is starting to set, Moreen enjoys the view for a bit then jumps off the cliff and into the ocean. She swims for about 2 miles around the island and rests on the beach a half-mile from their main beach. At the same time, Matt wonders where Moreen is and when she might return.

About an hour after the sun is down Moreen arrives at the spot where they are staying, and Matt asks, "Where you been?" Moreen responds, "Just roaming the island one more time before we leave, and I spent some time sitting up on the cliff" "O ok" Matt replies. They then both hang out on the beach for several hours into the night. The weather on this night was cooler than any other night but to both it as they sat by a fire and had some drinks. By midnight they were drunk and feeling tired. They took a dip into the ocean for a few minutes and then went right into the tent and off to sleep.

Matt wakes up after only 2 hours and its almost 3 AM. He tries to fall back asleep right away but can't. So, he gets out of the tent so he doesn't wake Moreen, sits on a stump, and has more beer to drink. Then around sunrise hours later, he goes back into the tent where he falls back to sleep.

After sleeping 9 hours, Moreen awakes and feels rested. With Matt still asleep she gets out of the tent and walks around the beach. She goes for a dip in the ocean water as the sky above is clear as hell. At around 1 PM Matt gets up and sees Moreen lying in the sand near the water. He joins her by laying beside her and they lie there for a few hours. Feeling hot, they get up and go for a dip into the water to cool off. After swimming for a few hours they have the last few drinks they have in the box and sit on the shoreline.

Matt and Moreen go for another swim as the sun is setting, and they stay in the water for a couple hours. They exit the water just before the sun is down and Matt starts a fire. After a few passing hours, they see a ship in the distance and it comes closer and closer to them until it docks 500 feet away from them. A man approaches them to tell them that he's there to help them out and will drop them off on the west coast of Florida. They then board the ship and are shown to a bedroom where they have clothes hanging there along with a nice size bed to sleep in. Right away they get into the bed and dose off to sleep.

Matt and Moreen wake up a few hours later when the ship is 2 hours away from Florida. The ship provides them with a meal to eat and some drinks. So, when the awake the get dressed, luckily the clothes provided fit them and they go up on the deck and eat. Then for the rest of the ride, they enjoy a few drinks.

By 3 PM eastern time the ship pulls in to Tampa, Fl. After getting off the ship Matt and Moreen get a bus to a local Bank of America, luckily Matt and Moreen kept their IDs with what little belongings they had and Matt was able to get some cash. Matt immediately got himself a new phone and then they went to stay in a hotel room.

Ch 8: Trying to Return to A Normal Life.

At 10 AM Matt and Moreen get up and within an hour leave the hotel. They take a bus to a rent-a-car place where Matt rents a car. They then load up on snacks and soda and Matt drives Moreen down to her university in Miami. After dropping her off, Matt goes to the nude beach until 6 that evening. After the beach, he goes to some nightclubs in Miami beach and gets a hotel room.

By the time Moreen showed up at college, she had 12 days before classes started. She opened a bank account, and talked to her social worker in Nevada, she got $12,000 to help her out and that did not need to go to her school because she was on a basketball scholarship. She started classes and had a long journey through her college career. Matt helps Moreen set up her dorm and orders things for her that she will need. By 9 PM that night Matt leaves her dorm after being instructed to by campus security.

After leaving Miami, Matt drove for a while up I95. He stopped at a gas station near Daytona and met some nice young guy who needed a ride. So, Matt drives him 30 minutes to where he needs to go and then goes to a hotel as he is tired and it's midnight.

At 8 the next morning, he eats the complimentary breakfast and spends time talking with other travelers, and then hits the road. Matt then drives up I95 for 8 hours and by 8 PM he gets a room at a hotel on the South Carolina coast. After getting situated in the hotel Matt looks for a bar. He finds one up the road from the hotel and hangs out there for a few hours. Matt meets a young lady there and they talk for hours about life and their careers and at the end of the night, when the bar closes, they go their separate ways. By 3 AM Matt is back at his hotel room where he right away goes to sleep.

Hours later at 10 the next morning he gets back on the road. As Matt drives he calls his superiors, he explains what happened in hopes of still having his job. They tell him he might, but they would talk about it further in the office when he gets back. After 7 hours of driving that day, he reaches his home in New York City. He takes the rental car to a retailer and Ubers his way to his apartment.

Matt spends the weekend in his apartment relaxing and getting himself ready to go back to work the following week. After spending 2 days at home he feels refreshed and goes back to the office. On his first day back, he works for a few hours and then has a meeting with his superiors. He explains everything that happened and the meeting lasted a couple hours. In the end, he was able to keep his job but gave up any vacation time for the next couple of years and also had to extend his employment contract.

Matt works his ass off for a long while 5 to 6 days a week. Most days he has his lunch break in the courtyard and sees the same people eating lunch every day. One day after a few months this woman, named Jazmin approaches him, it is someone he sees a lot. They start talking during lunch and after work, they go to a bar together. They hang out there for a while as it's a Friday night and then they go their separate ways. When they see one another Monday at lunch they sit together and talk further. After a few months of them sitting together and talking at lunch, they start dating.

Matt and Jazmin date for a year and their relationship seemed perfect. So when Jazmin dumped Matt it was a big shock to not only Matt but also his close friends. The break-up devastates Matt and he becomes very depressed for a while. For a few months, he does nothing but go to work. He eventually pulls himself out of his depression and starts hanging out with friends again.

When Matt has his vacation 5 months later, he goes to Miami Beach in the middle of the summer for 9 days. He stays in a hotel on South Beach and parties a lot in the evening. On his 3rd day, he is chilling at a nude beach. Within an hour after him sitting there, he sees a girl walking in his direction. As the girl gets closer he says "Moreen?" she stops and is sort of surprised to see Matt again.

Moreen and Matt hang out together on the beach from about 3 that afternoon until the sunset. When they leave the beach, they make a plan to meet a couple hours later at a bar in South Beach. They then have a great night together and catch up more. At the end of the night they go their separate ways and through Matts last week on vacation they hang out once more. On his last night, Moreen hangs out in his hotel room until he leaves the next morning for his flight back home.

Made in the USA
Middletown, DE
05 May 2022